When I saw it was Angelique in my bed I relaxed and holstered my gun. "What are you doing here?" I asked.

"Waiting for you," she said.

"What the hell for?"

She dropped the sheet to her waist and I saw she was naked. Her figure was full and ripe. She wasn't the little girl I had taken her for earlier; she was a full-grown woman.

"What do you think?" she said by way of answering my question.

I approached the bed slowly. "Remember," I told her, "I'm a wounded man."

"You just come here," she said, holding out her arms. "I'll make you feel better."

THE GUNSMITH

3

THE WOMAN HUNT

J.R. ROBERTS

CHARTER
NEW YORK

A Division of Charter Communications Inc.
A GROSSET & DUNLAP COMPANY
51 Madison Avenue
New York, New York 10010

THE GUNSMITH #3: THE WOMAN HUNT

An Ace Charter Original

First Ace Charter printing: March 1982

Published simultaneously in Canada

Manufactured in the United States of America
2 4 6 8 0 9 7 5 3 1

THE GUNSMITH

3

THE WOMAN HUNT

To the other Clint—The Man With No Name and The High Plains Drifter.

Prologue
OKLAHOMA, 1858

I was twenty-five years old back then, and had been a lawman for only five years or so. I had a lot to learn, and I was still very eager to learn it.

I had been deputy sheriff in Stratton, Oklahoma for eighteen months and elections were coming up. The sheriff at that time was Jim Bailey, but Old Jim was due for retirement and he had no intentions of running again. I did.

Her name was Jennifer Sand and she was twenty years old. She had long red hair, an upturned nose, and a wide mouth with full lips. She had small, perfectly rounded breasts, a waist I could almost encircle with my hands, and long, lovely legs. I soon found out that she was old-fashioned, a lady, and I found myself acting like a gentleman for the first time since coming West. It had never been necessary before.

I was just beginning to think about asking her to marry me when Harve Bennett rode into town. Bennett was a gunhawk, one of the best—or so his reputation went. It was Old Jim who recognized him when he rode in, and he came into the office to tell me about it.

Jim leafed through the Wanted posters and finally

brought one out. He handed it to me and I scanned it.

Harve Bennett, wanted for robbery in Missouri. He was about thirty-five, five-ten, brown hair, clean-shaven.

"Wonder what he wants here?" Jim said.

I shrugged.

"He's wanted in Missouri, not here, so let's keep an eye on him and maybe we'll find out," I suggested.

"That's for you to do, young fella," Jim told me. "Your eyes are better than mine, anyways."

He was standing at the bar when I entered the saloon, looking into a glass of whisky. I walked to the bar, careful not to stand too close to him, and ordered a beer from George, the bartender.

"You want to talk to me, Deputy?" Bennett asked without looking at me.

"Why would I want to do that?" I asked.

Still not looking at me he said, "Oh, I don't know. Me being a stranger in town and all, I just thought maybe you'd want to talk to me about something."

"You got it wrong, friend," I told him, "I just came in here for a beer."

He turned his head slowly in my direction and our eyes locked for a moment. A small, grim smile showed on his face, then he turned his head away and finished his whisky.

"I'm going to the hotel," he told me, "then I'm coming back here to find a poker game. You can follow me there, or wait for here." Then he added, "Just don't crowd me, Deputy."

I watched him walk out the batwing doors and then realized that we had been the center of everyone's attention.

I finished my beer and told George, "Give me another one."

Setting it down in front of me he asked, "Who was that, Clint?"

"Harve Bennett. Ever heard of him?"

"Yeah, I guess I have. Never seen him before, though."

"Neither have I," I told him. I drank my beer and put the empty glass down on the bar. "If he comes back here, like he says he will, send someone over to find me, okay?"

"Sure, Clint, sure."

"Thanks."

A kid brought the word over later for two bits. When I entered the saloon I saw that Bennett was indeed playing poker, and doing very well for himself. Too well, judging from the reactions of one of the players, a cowhand who seemed to be down to his last few dollars. It looked like fireworks if Bennett took another hand.

After some raising back and forth, the cowhand snapped, "Look, friend, you know yore not gonna beat me this hand, so why you tryin' to make me look like a horse's ass? I'm gonna raise you again, damn it!" And with that he pushed the last of his money into the pot.

I think the only reason Bennett didn't raise him back was because he knew the man had no more money.

"I call."

"Hah!" the cowhand shouted, throwing his hand down. "A flush right from the deal, damn it! Beat that!" he said, triumphantly.

"Sorry, friend," Bennett drawled, and laid his full house on the table.

The cowhand's face went red and he jumped up yelling, "By God, you cheat!"

He was gonna go for his gun and get himself killed. I could see it.

"Hold it!" I shouted.

My shout stopped his hand halfway to his gun.

"My friend, if you go for that gun, I'm going to have to go for mine. If I do that, you'll be dead."

"B-but he's a card cheat. He took all my money!"

"He *won* all of your money," I corrected. "If you can't afford to lose you shouldn't be playing. Ease your hand away from your gun and go on home."

He looked around at the crowd that was watching him, then drew himself up and walked out as quickly as he could without running.

Bennett reached for his money, folded it up and tucked it away in a pocket. Then he stood up, turned and walked to me. I was about to say something when suddenly he backhanded me across the mouth, knocking me back against the bar, causing my hat to fly off and my ears to ring. Dimly, I was aware of him saying, "Don't ever put your nose in my business again, sonny."

By the time my ears and eyes cleared, he was gone. My ears burning from the embarrassment, I retrieved my hat and walked out, ignoring the stares and muttered comments.

Jenny had a room at Mrs. Werth's boarding house and I had promised to meet her there for dinner. I was a few minutes late, which was unusual in itself, because I was usually very early when going to meet her. She knew right away something was wrong. There was also the bruise that had appeared as a result of the blow Bennett had struck.

"What happened, Clint?" she asked with concern, touching the bruise with her fingers.

We went to the parlor and sat on the couch and I told her what had happened, and what I was thinking of doing.

"Why do you have to do anything?" she asked.

"Jenny, I have to live in this town, I have to have the respect of the people. I can't let something like this just go without taking some kind of action."

"Have you talked to Sheriff Bailey about this?"

"No, I haven't."

"Well, isn't it his decision to make?"

"No, it's mine."

"Well, what am I supposed to do if this man kills you just because your pride is hurt?" she demanded. "Clint, listen. Talk to the sheriff. If he agrees with you, then the both of you can go after this man together."

When I agreed to do that much she threw her arms around me and hugged me, and at that point someone banged loudly on the door.

"Who could that be?" she asked.

It was George, the bartender at the saloon.

"You better come quick, Clint," he said, breathlessly.

"What's the matter, George?"

"That gunny, Bennett? He just shot down Old Jim Bailey."

"Oh, no," Jenny breathed from behind me.

I went numb for a moment, then turned to Jenny, whose eyes were wide with horror and said, "Now it *is* up to me."

I had them move Jim to the undertaker's, but before that I removed his badge.

"I'm sorry, Jim," I told him, "but I need this more than you do right now."

I had to have it on when I killed Bennett, because it would be like having Old Jim with me—which was what Jenny wanted.

Only she didn't see it that way. When she saw me with the sheriff's badge on my chest, she reacted violently.

"I cannot just sit here and wait for word that you've been killed. Clint, if you ride out to look for Bennett, I won't be here when you get back."

"Jenny—"

"I mean it, Clint. I love you, but I won't be here."

The town started buzzing as Bennett and I rode down the main street. They were impressed that he wasn't tied, or slung over his saddle. I directed him to the jail, and walked him in without taking my gun from my holster.

The fact that I needed a bath was brought home to me

when Mrs. Werth opened her door to my knock, then gave me an outraged look and a loud sniff.

"I'm sorry, Mrs. Werth, I know I must be a sight, but I wanted to talk to Jenny as soon as I got back."

"Too late for that, young man," she told me.

"Where is she, Mrs. Werth. If I could just talk to her—"

"I said it was too late, and that's what I meant, Clint Adams. She left town a week ago."

I had never imagined that Jenny was serious when she said she wouldn't be there when I returned.

But she had, and she was gone. On top of that, Harve Bennett never arrived at the state prison. He escaped on the way. He was free, and now it had been all for nothing.

OKLAHOMA
1871

1

I was back in Stratton, starting a search I should have begun years ago. Old Jim Bailey was thirteen years dead, and Harve Bennett was barely dead two weeks. I hadn't killed him, but I had been there and I had been part of the circumstances leading up to his death. His death led to my decision to start my search for Jenny Sands, thirteen years too late.

The town of Stratton, Oklahoma hadn't changed much since I'd last seen it. I dropped my rig off at the livery stable, then mounted Duke, my big black, and rode him to the saloon. The livery boy was a stranger to me; I dropped some extra money on him so he'd remember me and take special care of Duke when I brought him back.

The saloon had the same old sign hanging over the entrance, saying simply: *Saloon*. I knew it was the same sign because it still had the three bullet holes inside the first "O," which I had put there on a bet. That was another way I'd changed over the years; back then I had been eager at times to show my prowess with a sixgun.

11

These days I used it only when necessary.

I tied Duke to the hitching rail and went on into the saloon. The bartender was unfamiliar to me. I stepped up to the bar and ordered a shot and a beer.

"Just ride in?" he asked.

"Yep."

"You'll like Stratton," he told me putting down one glass, then the other. "It's a nice little town."

"It looks little," I told him.

"Well, that may be, but we're growing," he assured me.

"Is that a fact?" I asked, then took my shot and beer to a corner table.

It was early in the day, before noon, and I was the only one in the saloon. My initial intention had been to go immediately to Mrs. Werth's boarding house—or what used to be Mrs. Werth's boarding house—where Jenny had lived. But when I was approaching town I got a little apprehensive. What if Mrs. Werth no longer lived there? She was the only chance I had of obtaining even a hit of Jenny's intentions when she had left Stratton. If Mrs. Werth was gone—or dead—the trail would be dried up before I got started. Rather than face that possibility, I decided to have a drink or two, then grab a shave, bath, and a room. If Mrs. Werth did indeed still live in town, I wanted to look presentable when I called on her. She was an upstanding woman and wouldn't take kindly to my coming into her house directly from the trail.

A few men ambled into the saloon as noon came and went, but I didn't recognize any of them. I was beginning to suspect that the entire population of the town had changed, when Marty Daniels walked in.

Marty had been a part-time jailer for Old Jim and me back then, and he usually worked for the price of a drink. From what I could see the years hadn't been kind to him. He was near sixty, and his face and body had bloated up some. His drinking habits had taken their toll.

"Marty!" I called out. He was arguing with the bartender about his credit.

He squinted in my direction, then started towards me, trying to make out my face. It took him a few moments, but when he finally placed me, his face lit up in a smile.

"Who's that?" he asked, coming closer still. "Is that Clint Adams?"

"It's me, Marty. Sit down and have a drink with me," I invited. I called for the bartender to bring over a bottle and another glass.

"You give this old coot free drinks, Mister, and he won't—" he started to say as he put the bottle down, but I cut him off before he could get much further.

"Marty and me are old friends, bartender. Do you see anything wrong with one friend buying a drink for another?" I asked him, looking him straight in the eye.

He looked away from me and muttered, "Hell, don't make no never mind to me . . ." and walked back to the bar, still muttering.

I poured Marty a good stiff one and asked, "How have you been, Marty?"

"Ah, times have been better, Clint. You remember."

"Oh, I can remember better times, Marty," I assured him, as he downed the whisky in one swallow. He shivered as the rotgut hit bottom, then pushed his glass forward again. I poured him another drink and asked, "Anybody I know still live in town, Marty?"

"Sure, Clint, sure. There's still a few familiar faces in town, but it ain't like it used to be, not like it was thirteen years ago."

He wasn't as far gone as he appeared if he could peg exactly the last time I was there.

"The saloon and livery got new owners," he went on,

"but some of the other stores have the same people running them." He stopped to inhale half his new drink.

"You've built up quite a reputation for yourself, Clint. Call you The Gunsmith, don't they?"

"Some have, yeah."

"I remember when you first got interested in guns," he said, thinking back. "Always takin' them apart and puttin' them back together again." He finished his second drink and asked, "What brings you back our way, Clint?"

"I'm trying to pick up a cold trail, Marty," I told him.

He frowned. "I never heard nothin' about you bein' a bounty hunter."

"I'm not a bounty hunter, Marty, but I am hunting, that much is true," I explained. "That's all I want to say right now, if it's all right with you."

"Hey, kid," he said, "anything you did was always okay with me, you know that. You don't want to say more, that's good enough for me."

I poured him another and he polished it off. I was ready to pour again, but he turned his glass upside down, saying, "That's enough for breakfast, Clint. I thank you."

"My pleasure, Marty."

He stood up and stayed there, looking at me for a few moments more.

"You sure have changed a lot, boy," he said, finally. "A whole lot."

"And not just where you can see it, Marty," I told him.

"That's what I meant," he replied, then turned and shambled out through the batwings.

I finished my beer and had another shot. Even though I paid for the whole bottle, I took the rest back to the bar and said, "Here you go," setting it down. "You can sell the rest to somebody else."

He gave me a dirty look, but took the bottle anyway.

"Who's the sheriff in this town?" I asked him.

"Bates, Andy Bates," he answered. The name meant nothing to me, so I asked him who the mayor was.

"That's be Mayor Catch."

"Old Ben Catch is still mayor?" I asked. "He must be crowding seventy by now."

"Pretty near. You sound like you know him."

"Yeah, I did, once. Thanks."

"Yeah, sure."

I went outside, unhitched Duke and walked him down to the sheriff's office. I figured I'd check in with the local law and get a look inside the old office at the same time.

The sheriff looked more like a farmer than a lawman. He was tall and thin and he wasn't wearing a gun—at least, he didn't have a gunbelt on when I entered the office, and I didn't see one hanging anywhere. There was an old Henry rifle leaning up against the side of his desk however.

"Sheriff Bates?" I asked as I entered.

"Can I help ya?" he asked, without standing up from behind his desk.

Jesus, I thought, the same desk, too.

"My name's Clint Adams, Sheriff. I just got into town and wanted to check in with you."

He squinted his eyes at me and asked, "You wanted for something?"

"No, I'm not wanted," I assured him.

"Adams," he said. "Seems to me I've heard that name before." He screwed his homely face up tight and I took that to mean he was concentrating.

"I was a lawman for a while," I told him. "Started right here in Stratton, as a matter of fact."

"Uh-huh," he replied, looking unimpressed. He rubbed his long, stubbled jaw and asked, "You sure you ain't wanted for anything?"

"No, Sheriff, I'm not wanted for anything. You talk to Marty Daniels, or Mayor Catch, they'll tell you who I am."

While he thought about that, I looked over the office. It was virtually unchanged, except that everything was thirteen years older than it was the last time I saw it. Stratton hadn't gone forward or backward, it appeared. It had stayed exactly the same.

"I like to make it a habit to check in with the local law when I hit town, Sheriff. That's all I'm doing," I explained.

"Uh-huh," he said again, still looking at me hard, trying to remember if he'd ever seen my face on a wanted poster.

"You stayin' long?" he asked.

I shook my head.

"Just overnight, I hope. I should be finished with my business and ready to move out by morning."

"Well, just don't start no trouble," he warned, trying to look mean. I wondered how mean he would really be if there ever was trouble.

"Don't worry, I won't, Sheriff," I promised. "I'll even let you know when I'm ready to leave. How's that?"

"That's fine, just fine," he told me. He leaned back in his chair, as if satisfied that he'd performed his function as sheriff.

"Thank you for your time, Sheriff. I appreciate it," I said, heading for the door.

"Hey, uh, Adams," he called out before I could make it through the door.

"Yeah?" I asked with my hand on the knob.

"You sure you ain't wanted for anything?"

2

The meeting with the sheriff left a bad taste in my mouth. He was an insult to the office once held by Old Jim Bailey. Old Jim had less ability than half the lawmen I'd known over the years, but he understood his job. I was disappointed in the town of Stratton for having made Andy Bates sheriff.

I took Duke back to the livery and reminded the boy to take extra good care of him.

"Don't you worry, Mister," he told me, "this is the best lookin' animal I ever seen." Judging by his enthusiasm, I figured Duke was in good hands.

My next stop was the hotel.

"You still offer a bath and a shave?" I asked the desk clerk.

"Yes, sir!" he snapped back, "Right in back."

"Okay, fine. Have someone bring my gear up to my room."

"Of course, sir." This clerk looked like he might have been all of eighteen.

"Thank you," I told him, and left him an extra two bits.

Sitting in the bath I reflected on what I thought my aims were in searching for Jenny Sand. Killing Harve Bennett had closed a chapter in my life. Bennett had

17

killed Jim Bailey and cost me Jenny Sand. He had also
escaped after I had captured him and brought him back
to Stratton for the murder of Old Jim. There had been
a few occasions over the ensuing years when I wondered
what had happened to Bennett. Now he was dead, and
there were no more thoughts about him—only about
Jenny, a re-opened chapter in my life. Now that I was
thinking about her again, I felt I had to find her, or at
least attempt to find her, so that I could get on with the
rest of my life.

I had stayed too long in the bath, and the water had
turned tepid. I dried off and got dressed, leaving my trail
clothes for the attendant to clean and then deliver to my
room. I gave him an extra two bits. I buckled on my
gunbelt, and left the hotel by the rear, intending to look
up Mrs. Werth. Before I realized what I was doing, I
found myself heading for Mayor Catch's office.

The last time I had seen Mayor Catch, I had ignored
him. It was after I returned to town with Harve Bennett.
The Mayor had approached me, saying how proud the
town was and all, but all I had on my mind was seeing
Jenny again. Even before that we'd never had many
dealings. I was just a deputy—in spite of the fact that I
had appointed myself sheriff after Jim's death.

I wondered if Catch would remember me at all.

He did.

I had no sooner entered his office than the old man
stood up and extended his hand.

"Clint Adams," he said.

"I'm surprised you remember me," I told him, taking
his hand.

"An old man has little left but his memories," he told
me, sounding terribly sad.

He was sad to look at, too. He was a shriveled-up
hulk of a codger. Once he had entertained real political
ambitions. Even thirteen years ago it had been evident

to everyone but himself that he would go no further. Now he finally seemed to have realized it himself.

"Sit down, Clint. Tell me what brings you to Stratton after so many years?"

I sat down and lied. "Just passing through, Mayor, that's all."

"Hmm. Let's see, the last time I saw you was when you brought that killer in—what was his name?" he asked, trying to remember.

"Harve Bennett."

"That's the one. He escaped later, didn't he?"

"Yes, sir."

"Wonder what ever happened to him."

There were several ways I could have put it but what I said was, "He was later brought to justice, Mayor."

"Well, that's good."

He took a handkerchief from his breast pocket and wiped away the seepage from his eyes.

"By you?"

"I was there," I said, hedging.

He nodded, saying again, "That's good. And what ever happened to that young lady of yours?"

"Jenny Sand? I really couldn't tell you, sir. I never saw her again after I left town to pick up Bennett's trail?"

"Oh, really? I thought that you might have left town to meet with her? You never saw her again?"

"No, sir, never again."

"That's a shame. A lovely girl, as I remember."

"Yes," I said, forming a picture of her in my mind. "She was lovely."

"I've followed your career, you know," he told me, catching me off balance with the statement, "as well as I could through the newspapers. It seems to me you established quite a reputation for yourself."

"I've only tried to do my job."

"Still a lawman?"

"Not anymore."

"Like to be?"

"I beg your pardon?"

"We need a sheriff, Clint."

"You've got one."

He made a face and said, "Andy Bates is not a law-man. We need a real lawman, Clint, or—" then he stopped short and looked down at his desk top. It was a few moments before he spoke again, and the despair in his voice was plain to hear.

"I don't blame you for not wanting to be sheriff of a dying town, Clint, and that's what Stratton is, a dying town, just as I am a dying man."

I didn't know what I could possibly say to him and, truth be told, I no longer wanted to be in the same room with him.

"I'm sorry I can't help you, Mayor," I told him, rising.

When I left the Mayor's office, I went straight to Mrs. Werth's boarding house. It was still standing, and like the rest of the town, it was virtually unchanged. I hoped Mrs. Werth still lived there.

I was feeling more nervousness than I had felt in years as I approached the front door. I took a very deep breath and knocked.

All the fears I had about Mrs. Werth having moved from town disappeared when she opened the door.

"Yes?" she asked. "Can I help you?"

Except for her white hair and a few more wrinkles, she looked the same as the last time I saw her, although she must have been in her mid-sixties.

"Mrs. Werth?" I asked, "Don't you remember me?"

A bemused expression crossed her face as she searched her memory.

"Now that you mention it—" she said, and then the

expression on her face froze.

"It's about time, Clint Adams," she scolded.

"I don't understand, Mrs. Werth."

"Come in," she told me, stepping back. She closed the door and led me to her sitting room.

"I've been waiting for you to realize what a wonderful girl you let get away from you, Clint," she explained.

"But Mrs. Werth, it's been thirteen years. Certainly you couldn't have still been expecting me?" I asked her, and she hit me right between the eyes with her answer.

"You came back, didn't you?"

She was right about that.

"You know, for the first few years, I couldn't wait for you to come back so I could tell you where Jenny was."

"That's—" I started, but she rushed right on without letting me get a word in.

"Then I swore if you came back I wouldn't tell you a thing, that if it took you that long to come to your senses, you didn't deserve to find her."

I waited for her to go on, and when she didn't I asked, "And how do you feel now?"

She looked at me for a few moments, then got up and walked over to a small writing desk in the corner. She opened the drawer and took something out, then walked back to me and handed it to me.

It was an envelope addressed to her, and I recognized the handwriting.

"That's the last letter I received from Jenny, Clint Adams. You can take it and be off. I still have no use for you, not after what you did to that poor girl. She cried the whole time you were off, until she finally decided to leave. I can't forgive—" she stopped short, as if needing a moment to compose herself. "I'm sorry, Clint, but I can't forgive you, even if she can."

"She can—what do you mean?"

"Take the letter and go. You'll understand when you

read it. Now please, leave my house."

I stood up and put the letter in my pocket, although I was anxious to open it and read it.

"I'm sorry you feel that way, Mrs. Werth—"

"Save your apologies for that sweet young girl, Clint Adams. Although she's a grown woman, now, and married, I hope, with tons of children."

"Goodbye, Mrs. Werth," I said. She didn't answer, or offer to show me to the door. I found it myself without too much trouble, and used it.

3

The letter had been mailed from a town called Red Sky, in Texas. It read this way:

> *Dear Mrs. Werth,*
> *I'm writing to tell you that I'm moving away from here. It hasn't turned out to be what I hoped for. I'll be moving on, and I'll let you know where I settle. You sounded so bitter towards Clint in your last letter. Try to forgive him, Mrs. Werth. I have.*
> > *Love,*
> > > *Jenny*

The letter was dated ten years ago.

I had waited until I got back to my room to open it, and now I stuffed it back in the envelope and put it away in my saddle bag.

The letter was ten years old, but Mrs. Werth said it had been the last letter she received from Jenny. Why hadn't she written again, as she said she would? It would have been so much easier. Now all I had to go on was that she had been in Texas ten years ago. I also knew now that she had forgiven me. If I had decided to look for her earlier, things might have been different, for her, and for me . . .

Thinking that way was useless. I went over to the livery to tell the boy to have Duke and my team ready to leave in the morning.

"I wouldn't leave tomorrow morning if I was you, Mister," the boy advised.

"Why's that?" I asked him.

"Come with me and I'll show you."

He took me to a back stall where he had put one of my team. He lifted one of the horse's rear legs to show me the bottom of the hoof.

"See there?" he asked, pointing. "He must have stepped on a pebble as you were coming into town. He's got the beginnings of a bruise."

"How do you know it happened coming into town?" I asked, bending down to inspect the mark.

"If he'd gotten it earlier it would be worse, from walking on it. As it is, he ain't had time to walk on it and make it worse. If you take him out in the morning, though, he won't go far before he'll pull up lame."

He dropped the foot and I looked at him. "What's your name?"

"Willie."

He was a tall, gangly kid with big shoulders but stringbean legs and arms.

"How do you know so much about horses?" I asked.

"Heck, I been around them all my life. My pa ran this livery till he died last year. I been working here since I was ten."

I looked a little closer at him and asked him, "What's your last name?"

"Parker."

"Was your old man Lonnie Parker?" I asked.

"You knew my pa?" he asked.

"Not all that well, but I knew him. I was a deputy

here thirteen years ago, when you were just a lad."

"What's your name?"

"Clint Adams," I told him. "How's my black?"

"Oh, Mister, he's just fine," he said, his eyes glowing at the mention of Duke. The big fella tended to do that to people. "He's over here," he added, taking me to another stall.

"Hiya, big boy," I greeted him, patting his massive neck with my right hand while he nuzzled my left.

"That horse sure loves you," the kid told me.

"We have a lot of respect for each other," I told Willie, rubbing Duke's big nose. "I'll see you tomorrow, big fella. Willie here's going to take good care of you."

"You can bet on that," Willie told Duke.

"I guess I'll be around another day or so, Willie—or do you think that bruise needs longer than that to heal?"

"No, Mr. Adams, I think you'll be able to leave day after tomorrow, with no problem."

"Good. I'll drop by tomorrow to see Duke."

"See you then."

When I left he was talking in a low voice to Duke but the big fella was probably ignoring him, which wasn't Willie's fault. That big horse just didn't have much use for anyone but me, and that was the way I liked it.

I decided to have myself a steak and then hit the sack. I was starting to feel the effects of the trip, and I didn't really enjoy the prospect of being stuck in Stratton for an extra day. I figured a long, leisurely dinner followed by a few drinks would take me into a good night's sleep and then it would be morning. I had no idea how I would kill an extra day in Stratton, but I'd worry about that when tomorrow came.

I went to the saloon for a before-dinner drink, and the place had filled considerably since I'd left that afternoon. As I entered I noticed that there was a lull in the conversation, and I thought I knew why. I never denied that I had earned something of a reputation over the past thirteen years, and it was obvious that word had gotten around that I was in town. I ignored the inquiring eyes and walked to the bar to order a beer.

When the bartender brought it I asked him, "Where's the best place in town to get a good steak?"

"Down the street, Mrs. Bright's Cafe. She makes the best steak in the state."

"Well, with a reputation like that I guess I don't have any choice but to try her out," I told him.

The bartender seemed more nervous than he had that morning. Someone must have been telling tales behind my back. His stares were making me nervous, so I finished my beer and left the saloon to go and find Mrs. Bright's.

The cafe turned out to be right where my favorite dinner spot had been when I lived in Stratton. In fact, Jenny and I ate there together often.

It was one of the few buildings that had been fixed up. It had received a recent coat of paint, a new front window, and new drapes—not to mention a new proprietress. The old one had been a woman named Bertha, who weighed about two-fifty and never ate anything but her own food, and lots of it. I wondered what Mrs. Bright would look like.

I went in and found a corner table, sat with my back to the wall, a lesson I learned from a good friend of mine. Bill always sat with his back to the wall, because he knew there were plenty of people who would shoot him in the back first chance they got. I didn't flatter myself that there were as many gunning for me, but it only takes one.

Half the tables in the place were empty, so it wasn't long before the waitress came over to see what I wanted. She was a little old to be waiting tables, I thought, but that was all she was a little old for. She was about thirty-two or so, tall, with a full-bodied figure and a handsome face that just missed being beautiful because of her jaw.

It was a bit too large, but considering the rest of the
package, that could be forgiven.

"Can I help you?" she asked.

"I've heard you serve the best steak in the state," I
told her.

"You've been talking to Mel," she said.

"Yeah, he's the one," I admitted.

She laughed, a hearty laugh from deep in her throat,
and said, "Well, I suggest you judge for yourself."

I told her that was just what I was going to do, and
then I watched her every step to the kitchen.

The steak lived up to the advertisement, and so did
the fixings that went with it. The service was excellent,
too, and by the time I was up to my coffee, the place had
emptied out enough for me to ask the waitress to join me
for a cup. She said she'd be happy to.

"That steak was all it was cracked up to be," I told
her.

"Thanks," she said, as if she'd cooked it. I let it pass.

"I used to eat here a long time ago," I commented.

"Did you live here?"

"For a while."

"What happened?"

I hesitated a long moment, then said, "I decided to
leave."

"Well," she said, "I won't push it if you don't want to
answer."

"Thanks."

She offered me a second cup and I said only if she'd
have one.

"If it won't get you in trouble with your boss," I
added.

"Don't worry," she assured me, "it won't." And went
off to fetch the two cups.

When she returned, I asked, "When did your boss buy
this place?"

She seemed to be amused by the question.

"A couple of years ago."

"From who?"

"Lady named Watson, Bertha Watson."

"Big Bertha," I commented, "always ate too much of her own food."

"That was the lady," she said, laughing.

"I haven't asked you your name," I told her.

"No, you haven't."

We waited each other out for a few seconds, then she smiled and said, "It's Laurie."

"Hi, Laurie, my name's Clint."

"I know, Clint Adams. Word's gotten around."

"Am I the only stranger in town?" I asked.

She laughed and said, "You're the only stranger we've seen in weeks. People generally ride around this town."

"Why's that?"

"I think you know."

I did. It was the smell. You could smell a dying town from a mile off, and nobody even liked to ride through one, let alone stop at it.

"Why do you stay?" I asked.

She shrugged.

"I've got nowhere else to go."

"This can't be the greatest job in the world," I told her.

"It's not just a job," she told me. "My name is Laurie Bright, Clint. I own the place."

I took a few moments to look embarrassed and then said, "I didn't mean to imply—" but she took me off the hook by laughing.

"Don't worry, Clint. I haven't taken offense at anything you've said."

"Good, I'm glad. Uh, now that we've established that your boss won't mind you sitting here with me, how about your husband?"

Her eyes lowered. "I've been a widow for some time now, Clint."

"I'm sorry," I mumbled, and suddenly things started to feel awkward. I finished my coffee and said, "Well, Mrs. Bright—"

"Call me Laurie, please," she told me.

"All right, Laurie. That was the best meal I've had in some time."

"Thank you. I do all the cooking myself and pride myself on doing it well."

"I don't think I've ever tasted better, Laurie, so you should be proud."

"Thank you, Clint."

I stood up and asked, "Is breakfast as good as dinner?"

"Try it and see," she suggested.

"I guess I will. Good night, Laurie."

"Good night, Clint."

At times, a lovely woman can intoxicate you even more than whisky, and I guess I was slightly affected by the loveliness of Laurie Bright when I left her cafe. As I passed an alley on my way to my hotel, my mind on Laurie Bright, I was not a hundred per cent alert. Before I knew it I had been pulled into the alley by someone and received a blow to the middle of my back. The air rushed out of my lungs and I fell to the ground.

When the first boot caught me in the side I knew I'd have to get up. As I struggled to my feet, I became aware that there were more than two of us in that alley.

When I had my feet back under me I launched myself in a sideways dive, throwing the length of my body across that alley. I felt myself fall across the chests of two men and the three of us went down. I couldn't make out faces, but I could see them in silhouette and I started throwing punches, most of which landed solidly. I was doing all right for myself, which is not easy when you're fighting two men, until they got smart and moved away from each other to opposite ends of the alley. Now they came back at me from both sides and as we traded blows they started to get the better of me, because I could only face one of them at a time.

Finally, they were starting to wear me down, I decided to go for my gun, and that's when I discovered that there were more than just the three of us in the alley. As my hand touched the butt of my gun, something cracked the back of the head, and I crumpled. I hit the ground and they started kicking again. I covered my head as best I could, but unfortunately, that left my ribs and belly open and they were taking advantage of that.

It took me a few seconds to realize that they had finally stopped.

"Can you hear me, Adams?" I heard a voice ask.

"Huh?" was all I could manage, but it was enough.

"Good. It ain't healthy for you to stay in Stratton, Adams. You leave in the morning, you hear?" The stranger nudged me with the toe of his boot for extra emphasis. "In the morning, Mr. Gunsmith, understand?"

I was about to answer when a boot collided with the side of my head, and I went out for a while.

4

I regained consciousness in a strange bed. I lay there, staring at the ceiling, until I got brave enough to move my head. When I did I found out whose bed I was in. I've been in worse places.

"How do you feel?" Laurie Bright asked, looking concerned.

"Give me a minute," I told her. I did a mental check, and found that I was all there, and everything still moved.

"I'm okay, I guess. How'd I get up here?"

"I found you after I closed up. I got a couple of men to carry you up here for me. Doctor's out of town, so I thought it best that I kept an eye on you."

"I appreciate it," I told her. I struggled to sit up. It was painful, but I made it. She propped a couple of pillows behind me and I leaned back.

"How's that?" she asked.

"Fine. Have you notified the sheriff?"

She snorted, an unladylike sound, but it made her feelings about the sheriff very obvious.

"I wouldn't bother talking to Andy Bates for any reason," she told me.

Having met Bates and formed a quick opinion, I didn't blame her.

"Did you see who did this to you?" she asked.

I shook my head.

"There were three of them, but it was too dark for me to see any faces."

I looked around the room. No mirror; unusual for a woman's room. I wanted to see what injuries I had sustained.

"What's the damage?" I asked her.

"Not much," she assured me. "You've got a bruise under your right eye. No cuts, no broken bones that I can see. And that scar under your left eye—but you've had that awhile, looks like. How do you feel?"

I checked myself out again. I was worried about my ribs, since they had absorbed the most punishment. I was bruised, there was no doubt about that, but there didn't seem to be any broken ribs, for which I was grateful. I didn't want injuries keeping me in Stratton any longer than was necessary. One day was mandatory, to give one of my horses time to recover, and that would be all I needed to find out who was behind the attack. I had ideas in that direction, already.

"Nothing feels broken," I told her.

"That's good," she said, getting up from her chair. She had a basin and a cloth, and must have been bathing my head while I was unconscious. "Now what you need is rest."

"Is this your room?" I asked.

"Yes, but don't worry about that. We're upstairs from the cafe, and I have extra rooms. I can stay in one of those."

I became aware of the fact that I was wearing absolutely nothing beneath the covers of her bed.

"Who undressed me?" I asked.

"I did," she answered easily. "I'm way past the age of being embarrassed by naked men."

"Not that far past."

"Thank you. You better rest now."

I was tired, and I agreed. She put out the table lamp and left, saying she'd see me in the morning.

I got set to go to sleep, then looked for my gun. It was on a chair by the window. I swung my legs out from beneath the cover and planted my feet on the floor. When I stood up and found that I wasn't going to fall, I staggered across the room for my gunbelt, then turned and made the long trip back. After hanging my belt over the bedpost for easy access, I got back in bed and almost immediately fell asleep.

Sometime later I became aware that someone else was in the room with me. I was laying on my back and to reach my gun all I had to do was reach up over my head, if it became necessary.

It didn't.

My visitor slid back the covers of the bed and climbed in beside me. She had big, firm, round breasts that fit easily into my hands, and I tweaked the nipples to life as she pressed the length of her body against mine.

"From the moment you walked into my place," she whispered in my ear, "I was wondering how to get you into my bed. Now that I have, I didn't want to miss my chance."

"You only had to ask," I told her, and the words were barely out of my mouth before her lips came down over mine. Her tongue came alive in my mouth, and her hands roamed my body. She was eager, no, *anxious,* and I was willing to oblige.

I turned her over and went to work on her breasts with my mouth, teasing and biting her nipples until she was moaning and writhing beneath me.

"Oh, God," she moaned, crushing my face against her chest. My right hand slid between her legs and found her

wet and waiting. She went crazy as my fingers slid inside
of her, and her hand darted between my legs, found
what she was looking for and grabbed on tight.

"I can't wait," she cried in my ear, "Oh, please, I can't
wait, Clint."

Never one to tease a lady, I slid my fingers from inside
of her and moved my body atop hers. She put her hands
between us, eager to guide me home. It was the easiest I
had ever slid into a woman.

"Oh, God, it's been so long," she whispered as I slid
in to the hilt. "It's been so very long."

Her hands came around and grasped my buttocks, as
if to drive me even deeper. Her hips began to move beneath me. It took us a few moments to find the rhythm,
but when we did we were perfectly attuned.

Her hands left my buttocks and moved over my back
as she used her nails, indicating the increasing heights of
her passion. I had her buttocks in my hand, and they
were so smooth and round that I was satisfied to let my
hands stay right there. Her breasts were great cushions
against my chest, her nipples feeling like two little stones
digging into my skin.

"That's it, that's it," she was saying over and over
again and when her time came I felt as if she were trying
to throw me off. But there was no danger of that.

Afterward she said, "You must think I'm shameless."

Massaging her breast while her head lay in the crook
of my arm I said, "Well, any woman who could undress
a man without feeling embarrassed—" but she grabbed
the flesh of my stomach and twisted before I could finish.

"Actually, I simply decided that I wanted to sleep in
my own bed tonight, and it was going to take more than
your presence here to stop me."

"Well, since I refuse to move I guess there's only one
thing for us to do," I told her.

I could feel her eyes as she looked at my face and said in a teasing tone, "Again?"

I guess I didn't need as much rest as either of us had thought.

5

The next morning I got adopted.

I was sitting in the kitchen of the cafe, being served breakfast by Laurie Bright, when a big red mongrel came into the room.

"He yours?" I asked her around a mouthful of potatoes and eggs.

"Nope," she said, looking over her shoulder to see who I was talking about. "He came around a couple of weeks ago and I fed him. He comes everyday for breakfast, and then we don't see him again." She scraped some ham and eggs into a plate and put it on the floor.

"Eggs, too?" I asked.

"He won't eat without them," she explained.

I watched as the dog walked over to the plate and began to clean it hungrily.

"Funny thing," she said.

"What?"

"He won't go near anybody, or let anybody touch him. He just comes around to eat."

"Sounds like he wants to be left alone," I told her. "He must be smarter than he looks."

"Is that what you want, Clint?" she asked.

"What?"

"To be left alone?"

"Most of the time, yeah, I guess so," I answered honestly.

She regarded me silently for a moment, then turned to the stove and said over her shoulder, "Ready for seconds?"

"Yeah, I'm ready," I said, then looking at the dog added, "and so's our friend."

"Oh, he may be your friend, but he's not mine," she told me, although she went ahead and gave him another helping. He backed away from the plate until she was through, then went back and began eating again.

"First time he came around I tried to pet him," she told me, scraping more ham, eggs and potatoes into my plate, "and he almost took my hand off."

"You left him alone after that, didn't you?" I pointed out.

"Oh, you don't have to hit me over the head twice to get me to understand something," she assured me. There was a double meaning in there somewhere, but I didn't go looking for it.

"Aren't you going to eat?" I asked.

"I've got to watch my figure," she told me. "Besides, I've got to get ready for the morning rush. You were going to leave today, weren't you?"

"I was, but I've got to give one of my horses an extra day's rest. He picked up a stone bruise on the way into town."

"What are you going to do today?"

"I've got some questions to ask," I told her.

"About last night?"

"That's right."

"Can't you let it go? You're leaving town tomorrow."

"That's why I've got to find the answers today," I told her.

Shaking her head she observed, "I don't know why you men always have to prove that you're men by doing something stubborn."

"Weren't you proving something last night?" I asked.

I saw her shoulders stiffen and she took a few moments to decide whether or not she should be angry. I got lucky, because she apparently decided not to.

"You have a point," she told me without looking at me.

Since I was finished with my breakfast and she had work to do, I decided that the best thing would be for me to be on my way. I put on my hat and stood up, feeling some stiffness in my side.

"How do you feel?" she asked, turning to face me.

"Fine. You're a good nurse."

"See you later?"

"I'll be around," I told her.

She smiled and said, "Good luck."

I started to walk out and stopped when I heard a tapping sound behind me. I turned and found the red mongrel following me. It was his nails hitting the floor that was making the sound.

"What's this?" I said aloud.

Laurie looked over and said, "Well, I'll be. It looks like he's taken to you, Clint. He's never followed anyone before. He always just finished his breakfast and bounded out the back door."

I looked at the dog and he was looking up at me.

"What changed your mind today, boy?" I asked him.

"Maybe he feels a kinship towards you," she suggested.

"I guess there's no harm in him following me," I told her. "He'll probably take off when he gets bored."

"Somehow, around you I doubt that'll happen," she commented, and went back to work.

My first stop was Mayor Catch's office, because I could only think of one thing that had happened since I got to town that might cause someone to send three guys after me. The mongrel followed me all the way to Catch's office, then plopped himself down outside the door when I went in.

"Catch," I said, closing the door behind me.

The old man looked up at me from his desk in surprise.

"Clint. I thought you'd have left town by now."

"If I had my way, I would have. I want to ask you a question."

"What question?"

"What kind of a sheriff has Andy Bates been?"

He stared at me a moment with wet, rheumy eyes. "He's an abomination. The man doesn't look like much, but don't underestimate him, Clint. He rules this town with an iron hand."

Another crooked law man. It never seemed to end. Put a badge on some men, and immediately they abuse the authority behind it.

"You're the Mayor, Catch, why don't you do something about it?" I asked.

I was startled when the old man began to cry.

"I'm afraid," he cried out. "I'm old, and I'm afraid."

I was embarrassed for him, and would have liked to walk out right there and then, but I needed the answer to one more question.

"Mayor, yesterday you offered me the job of sheriff. Did you tell Bates that you made that offer? Did you threaten him with it?" I asked.

He couldn't speak, so he just nodded his head. That told me what I wanted to know. Bates wanted to make sure I didn't have any ideas about staying on in Stratton as sheriff. It might have been a dying town, but it was the only one he had, and he wanted to keep control of it.

"What's he got, three deputies?"

He nodded again.

"Okay, Mayor," I said, and turned to leave.

"Adams," he called.

"Yeah."

"You've got to get rid of him for me—for the town."

"No," I said, shaking my head. "I don't, not for you and not for this town. I just want to let him know that he made a mistake sending his boys after me."

I went back outside and found the mongrel still waiting for me.

"You still here, Red?" I asked him. He looked up at me and stood his ground, as if that were his answer. "Well, c'mon, then, we're going over to see the sheriff."

Bates must have been watching out his window, because as I—as *we* approached his office, he came out cradling a rifle.

"Thought you'd be gone by now, Adams," he drawled. Yeah, he looked like a farmer, all right, but if he chose to carry a rifle rather than a handgun, he was probably good with it.

"I ran into an unexpected delay, Bates, but not the one you're thinking of."

"What's that mean?"

"I don't want your job, Bates. You were stupid to send those three cowboys after me last night. I'd like you to step down from there, Sheriff. Without the rifle, please."

He laughed.

"So you can gun me down?" he asked.

"No, not likely. When you drop your rifle, I'll unbuckle my gunbelt."

"You want to meet me hand to hand?" he asked, laughing again. His eyes were darting to the right and to the left, never settling on me. He was stalling, and I thought I knew why. If I was right, I was about to be caught in a crossfire. The signal would have to come from Bates, so I kept my eyes on him.

"Bates, either drop the rifle, or make your move," I told him.

His face hardened, because I was supposed to be unprepared when he did make his move. Now he was having second thoughts, but in the end his decision was the same.

As he started to bring the rifle around, everything slowed down, as it always did when I went for my gun. I was that much faster than him that I saw his rifle every inch of the way. He barely had it out of his arms when I plugged him right in the chest. I could hear some kind of commotion to my left—someone yelling and a dog growling—so I turned to my right. As I did I saw another man pulling his gun from his holster. I pulled the trigger and shot him in the head. I heard another shot and felt the breeze of a slug whooshing past my head. I turned to my right again just as a third man was about to fire. I shot him in the heart.

When I turned to the fourth man, he was already occupied. The mongrel had latched onto his gun hand with his teeth and the man was screaming in pain. He swung the dog from side to side, but Red refused to let the man's wrist go.

I walked to where the man was struggling with the dog.

"Make him let go! Make him let go!" he shouted at me.

"Were you one of the men in the alley last night?" I asked him.

"Make him let go!" he shouted again.

"Answer my question," I told him.

"Yes, yes, I was there, now call him off!"

"Who were the other two?"

"Those two you killed. It was them and me. Now for God's sake, call this dog off before he rips my hand off!"

"I don't know if he'll listen." I holstered my gun. "He's not mine. He's got a mind of his own."

"He's tearing my arm off! Please, make him stop!"

"Well, I'll give it a try," I told him. "Hey, dog!"

No response.

"Hey, that's enough, dog!" I shouted, with still no response. "Hey, Red, let him go!"

I was surprised when the dog turned the man's arm loose and trotted over to where I stood. The man fell to his knees, holding his wrist. From the looks of him, he'd never pull a trigger again.

I walked to Bates to check him out, but he was dead. Red sniffed at him and snorted. I checked the other two and they were dead also. Then I turned my attention to the dog and thought about him. Considering that the third man—the one who had been behind me—had gotten off a hurried shot, the fourth man might very well have gotten off a more deliberate one, had it not been for the dog. All things considered, that mongrel dog may well have saved my life.

"Red," I told him, "you can follow me around all you want." I pointed my finger at him and added, "That's enough reward for anyone, my friend."

He woofed at me, and I took that to mean that he agreed.

6

I stayed in the saloon the rest of the day playing poker. No one spoke to me except to call my bet, or raise it, or to fold. The mongrel sat next to my chair and growled when anyone walked past. After a full day of cards I left the saloon. The bodies had been cleared from the streets. I had a late dinner at Laurie Bright's, and then we spent another night together. Even that was strained. But, as she had said before, she did not want to waste the opportunity. She had been long widowed and was hungry for what we had those two nights. Still she knew I'd be moving on in the morning, and in all probability, was relieved.

I turned down breakfast in favor of an early start. I said goodbye to Laurie and thanked her for two pleasant nights.

When I got to the livery Duke was saddled and my team was hitched.

"How's his hoof?" I asked Willie.

"It's fine, Mr. Adams, just fine, and Duke is ready to go, too," he said, enthusiastically. "Thanks for letting me take care of him. I don't think I'll ever see a more beautiful horse."

"Thanks, kid," I told him, and gave him some of my poker winnings—a small part of them, that is.

I tied Duke off behind the wagon and climbed up behind the team. When I looked behind me, I could see that the mongrel had taken up a position next to Duke, and Duke didn't seem to mind. Even if the dog hadn't already saved my life Duke's recommendation would have been good enough.

I patted my pocket, where I had Jenny's letter. My next stop was Red Sky, Texas. I hoped there would be another clue there, even after ten years.

If I was lucky, my woman-hunt would continue from there, and not end.

**TEXAS
1871**

7

Red Sky, Texas was larger than Stratton, Oklahoma, but it was still a small town, especially by Texas standards. It was only about twenty miles from the northern border, too far north for me to have any serious worries about Comanches.

When I rode into Red Sky I could see that, although it was a small town, it was also a busy one. It was before noon, but already the streets were teeming. What had made Jenny move on?

I put up the rig and Duke at the livery, leaving as I always did some extra money with the livery man to take extra good care of the big black. Red, the mongrel, trailed along after me as I walked to the hotel to get a room. After I had registered, I had a question for the clerk.

"I need to talk to someone who lived here ten years ago," I told him. "Who would you recommend?"

"There are a lot of people who lived here ten years ago," he told me.

"Did you?"

"No, but—"

"Tell me someone who has."

He thought a moment, then said, "The preacher. The sheriff. Mr. Lang, the owner of the general store—"

"That's enough, thanks," I said, and started up the steps.

"Excuse me," he called out.

"Yeah?"

"That dog."

"What about him?"

"Well, he can't go up with you."

I looked at the clerk, then at Red, then back to the clerk.

"Then you tell him," I said, and continued up the steps. When I got to my room, Red was still behind me, so I guess the clerk didn't tell him— or Red didn't listen.

"I hope you didn't take a piece out of him?" I asked.

He yawned, as if to show me that his jaws were clean, and he hadn't taken a piece out of anyone in days.

"Good enough," I told him, and went into the room.

I dropped off my saddle bag, and then went in search of a bath and a shave. When I had that, I went back to my room to change clothes. That time when I came back down there was a man waiting for me.

"Mr. Adams," he addressed me.

"Yes?"

"I'm the hotel manager."

"Good for you."

"It's about your dog, sir."

"I don't have a dog," I told him.

"Uh—" he stammered, pointing behind me. Red didn't like being pointed at, so he growled and showed his teeth.

"Oh, him?" I asked, turning and looking at the big mongrel. "He's not mine."

"He's not?" the manager asked, then looked at the clerk.

"He follows him around everywhere," the clerk said, by way of explanation. The manager looked back at me.

"Well, that's true enough, but that doesn't mean I own him. I have no control over him. He's his own dog. If you don't want him to go upstairs, tell him yourself," I suggested.

The manager looked at Red again, who growled at him again. The manager backed off, then started yelling at the clerk.

"What's wrong with you, it isn't even the man's dog. What are you calling me for—"

That was all I heard because I walked out while it was still going on.

Red followed me.

I went to the saloon for a drink before looking for one of the people the clerk had mentioned. The sheriff would probably be the best man to ask.

As I went through the batwing door, Red plopped himself down outside.

Too many people inside, I guessed.

"Beer," I told the bartender. I used half of it to wash away my thirst and then asked him who the sheriff in the town was. I usually asked this question when I entered a town, because often it would turn out to be someone I knew, but not in this case.

"His name's Case," the bartender told me, "Jim Case."

"Been sheriff long, has he?"

"About twelve years, I guess. I've only been here three or four, myself, but from what I hear Case has been here about twelve," he explained.

"Thanks," I said, and finished my beer. I was about to turn and leave when someone shouted into the saloon.

"Hey, Cal Mason's gonna use a mongrel dog as target practice," the voice called, and a few people started for the doors. Since I only knew of one mongrel dog outside, I hurried to the doors myself. When I got outside, Red was just where I left him.

"First I'll take out one eye," a man was saying, "then before his head hits the street, I'll shoot out the other."

The speaker was a man of about twenty-eight, with a gun on each hip, worn low. He was flanked by a number of other men who seemed to hang on his every word. Several townspeople had gathered to watch the show.

"Stupid dog," I scolded him. "What were you going to do, just sit there and let him shoot your eyes out?"

Red looked up at me as if to say, you wouldn't let that happen, now would you?

"No, I wouldn't."

"Hey, Mister, better stand clear of that hound," called the man with the two guns.

"I don't think so," I told him.

He looked at his friends, amused, and then said, "Well, then, spread your legs wide and I'll shoot his eyes out between them."

"I still don't think so, friend."

Now he wasn't so amused.

"Mister, you better move away from that dog," he warned, trying to sound menacing.

"Look son," I said. "Shooting the eyes out of a dumb dog, that's no way to put on a show for these people. It's too easy. Now try shooting my eyes out, there's a show."

"Mister, I think you're plumb loco," he commented.

"I'll tell you what, though. You better hope that you're not too fast with those pretty guns of yours."

That confused him.

"What do you mean, not too fast?"

"Well, if you're slow, see, I'll be able to wing you, without doing too much damage, but if you're fast— well, if you're fast I won't have all that much time to take aim, and I'll just have to kill you."

He wet his lips and darted his eyes around nervously.

"Mister, I can shoot the eye out of a fly at a hundred yards. I can plug a two bit piece on the fly, I can—"

"That's all fine, son, but I can kill a man at fifteen feet, and you're just about the right distance from me. Now either you go for those guns of yours, or you turn around and start walking. The choice is yours."

My own opinion was that he'd go for the guns. I had made it too difficult for him to back down, and even though he was nervous, all he could do was draw. I hoped he wasn't too fast, because what I had told him was true enough. If he cleared leather faster than I figured he could, I'd have to kill him.

He was getting encouragement from his friends to draw, and I was just standing there waiting for him to make up his mind when another, louder voice sang out over the others.

"I'll kill the first man who goes for his gun," it said in a deep, rumbling bass.

The kid froze up and looked around for the source of the voice. I let him locate it while I kept my eyes tight on him. Don't ever take your eyes off a man unless you're damn sure he's not going to draw.

"Sheriff—" the kid said, and a big man stepped forward from the crowd. He was big all over, with a barrel chest and legs like tree trunks. He wore one gun strapped to his left hip, and it looked well worn, as did he. The star on his chest told me that this must be Sheriff Jim Case, and he looked like a man who would do just what he said he would. The gun on his hip was a big .44 Colt Walker, probably the only gun that wouldn't come apart in his ham-sized hand. Right now that giant mitt rested on the butt of the gun, ready to pull it at a moment's notice. Somehow I got the distinct impression that the big man knew how to use it, too.

He took up a position between us and asked, "What's this all about, Franklin?"

The kid, Franklin, said, "We was just having some

fun, Sheriff, and all of a sudden this yahoo wants a gun-fight."

"That true, Mister?" the Sheriff asked me.

"Not exactly, Sheriff. I think if we disperse this crowd I could explain things in your office."

He stared at me hard a moment, then realized the wisdom of my words and nodded.

"Franklin, you and your friend move along. The rest of you, back to whatever you were doing." He turned to me and said, "Stranger, you want to follow me to my office?"

"My pleasure, Sheriff."

I followed him down the street to his office, where he gestured to a chair, and sat himself behind his desk.

"You want to tell me what happened out there?" he asked. "Or maybe you'd like to start with your name?"

"My name is Clint Adams, Sheriff."

"Adams, huh? Yeah, I've heard of you," he told me, but I couldn't tell from his tone whether what he heard was good or bad. "I guess Franklin's lucky I stepped in when I did."

"How good is he?" I asked.

"Oh, he's pretty good at trick shooting, but he wouldn't have been a match for you."

"Then I'm glad you stepped in, too."

"What was it about, anyway."

"A dog."

"A dog?"

"Mongrel that followed us over here."

"Is he yours?"

"Not exactly. He's kind of adopted me and we've ended up looking out for each other. Franklin wanted to show off by shooting his eyes out."

He blew air out of his mouth in disgust. "That damn kid and his guns. He's going to get himself killed one of these days, and I don't want it happening in my town."

"Who is he?"

"He's nobody, but his pa's one of the biggest ranchers hereabouts. I'm going to have to have a talk with him about his son."

That was none of my business, so I let it drop.

"Sheriff, I'd like to tell you why I'm in town," I told him.

"Fine, I'd like to know why a noted lawman—"

"Ex-lawman," I corrected.

"Ex-lawman, then, has come to my town."

I explained my reasons for coming to his town, that I was trying to get a line on a girl who had lived worked there ten years ago.

"Why?"

"She, uh, was somebody I knew thirteen years ago, and I'd like to see if I can find her."

He shrugged.

"Well, I guess your reasons for that are none of my business. What was her name?"

"Jennifer Sand."

He frowned and repeated the name a couple of times.

"Jennifer Sand, and you say she lived here ten years ago?"

"Well, she sent some letters from here ten years ago, and the last one said she was leaving town."

"Well, ten years is a long time. If you let me think about it I might be able to come up with something for you. I assume that aim now is to find out where she was going when she left here?"

"That's right."

He nodded, and got up from his chair. That seemed to be a signal for me to leave, so I rose, also.

"As I said, let me think about it and I'll get back to you. You have a room at the hotel?"

"Yes."

"I guess you don't want to stay in town any longer than necessary, so I'll try to come up with something fairly quick."

"I've got a few other people to talk to, but I appreciate you doing what you can."

"I'll be in touch."

"Thanks."

"Try to stay out of Franklin's way, okay?"

"I'll do my best," I promised. "I'm not looking for any trouble while I'm here."

"Good."

I went out and told Red, "Come along, stupid. And let's try not to get shot."

8

I gave the afternoon to making rounds, looking for ten-year-long residents.

The preacher turned out to be a man eighty years old and hard of hearing. He had trouble remembering what happened yesterday, let alone ten years ago. All I got after twenty minutes with him was a headache because I had to shout to be heard.

Mr. Lang was about fifty. His wife apparently kept him on a short leash. When I mentioned Jenny Sand, he looked around quickly to see if Mrs. Lang was within earshot, and I thought sure he was going to give me something I could use. Instead, he claimed not to have known anyone by that name, ten years ago or ever. I sensed he was lying, but I didn't press him right there and then. I figured I'd wait and see what Case came up with first.

At a few other places in town, I questioned owners and workers, but even those who were there ten years ago claimed never to have heard of anyone named Jenny Sand.

All the talking had made me thirsty, but I wanted to make one more stop before I went for dinner and a few drinks.

The schoolhouse.

When I thought of it, I wondered why I hadn't gone there first, considering that Jenny had taught school in Stratton.

The schoolteacher in Red Sky was a tall, thin young man of twenty-five. He said that he had been teaching school there for about three years, and had never heard of Jenny Sand. He told me that the person who had been teaching there before him was a woman, but that she was elderly, approaching sixty. I thanked him and headed for the saloon. As had been the case the entire day, Red was on my tail. He dropped himself down right outside the saloon and I looked around to see if there was any sign of the kid, Franklin. Then before I went inside I hunkered down next to that dog and said, "Dog, you better take good care of yourself while I'm inside. If you do, I'll bring you out a piece of steak, or something. All right?"

He stared at me with his big brown eyes, and I had the feeling he understood every word.

I asked the bartender what I could get to eat, and he said stew or steak. I took the steak. It wasn't as good as Laurie Bright's had been, and I decided halfway through to let Red finish it.

"Sorry, Red, no eggs," I told him. He'd been eating with me on the trail since we left Stratton, so he was used to having no eggs. He went right to work on the meat.

I went back in and ordered another beer, sat back and waited for a poker game to develop. I didn't have to wait long.

"Mind if I sit in?" I asked when four men arranged themselves around a table.

"Sure, stranger. Five-handed's better than four."

After a short while I realized I couldn't lose playing those four men even if I wanted to. In fact, I had to be careful not to win too much.

"Looks like I can't buy a winner tonight," one of them said, throwing in his hand.

"Guess I'm lucky," I replied.

After another half an hour I decided to quit for the evening. Once I left, one of them would have to start winning.

"Gentlemen, thanks for the game," I said, rising.

"I'm not sorry to see you go," one of them said.

"I am. He's got all my money, and yours," another commented.

"Yeah, but with him gone, I can get healthy off of you," the first one said.

"Hah, that'll be the day."

I bought a bottle at the bar to take back to my room with me, sidestepped a couple of streetwalkers and went out through the batwings to find Red waiting for me.

"What did I ever do to deserve you, I wonder?" I asked him.

He didn't answer, so I figured I'd never know.

"Let's go, Red. Time to hit the sack."

We started off down the street to the hotel, and I made myself especially aware of the alleyways that we passed, not wanting a replay of the incident in Stratton —although I had no good reason to believe that there might be one.

Even so, an alley was again the location of an attack, only this time it wasn't from up close. My instincts saved me, because I heard the shot a split second before someone else might have. I ducked, and the bullet imbedded itself in the side of a building, sending splinters of wood flying. A second shot echoed, and I was rolled into the alley. I felt some pain on the side of my face, but I kept moving to avoid making any kind of a target out of myself.

I stopped rolling with my back again the building, gun in hand, but I couldn't see anything to shoot at. I stayed crouched down, waiting and listening, and Red came over to see if I was okay.

"You okay, boy?" I asked without touching him. He didn't seem to have been hit, but then the shots were aimed much higher and he hadn't been in any real danger.

"Go sit over there," I told him, waving my free hand to the opposite end of the alley. I guess he was satisfied that I was okay because he did as I asked.

Two shots were all that had been fired, and I didn't expect that there would be anymore to follow, so after a few more moments I stood up and holstered my gun.

Now someone had gotten mad enough to shoot at me and I hadn't even been offered a job!

9

"Are you sure you didn't see anything?" Case asked while the town doctor bandaged my cheek.

"I couldn't see a thing, Sheriff. It was dark and whoever fired must have done it from across the street."

"He okay, Doc?"

"He's fine. Some wood chips sliced into his cheek. He was lucky."

"Yeah, damned lucky, I'd say. Well, I'll have to go out and pick him up."

"Pick who up?" I asked, puzzled.

"Why, Franklin, of course. He's the only one you've had a run in with since you hit town, ain't he?

"Yeah, but that doesn't mean he shot at me."

"Well, you tell me who else might have done it."

"I don't know."

"Then he's my only suspect, and I'm picking him up," he told me.

"You do your job the way you see fit, Sheriff," I told him, standing up and reaching for my gunbelt, "but I think you're jumping to a hasty conclusion."

"That may be so," he conceded, "but we'll know more when I talk to young Franklin."

I strapped on my gunbelt and reached for my hat.

"What do I owe you, Doc?" I asked. He told me and I paid him.

"Want a drink?" Case asked.

"I want some sleep," I answered.

"C'mon, I'll walk you to your hotel."

We started for the hotel and Red fell in behind us.

"You find out anything for me?" I asked him.

"Nope, nothing yet, and I haven't remembered her yet, either. I hear you been asking around town."

"That's right."

"Anybody remember?"

"Nobody. I thought one man might have remembered, but just when I thought he might tell me, he denied it."

"Who was that?"

"Mr. Lang, at the general store."

"Harry Lang," he said, and started laughing, shaking his head. "That is the most henpecked man I ever did see. Even if he knew your Jenny Sand, he wouldn't admit it. He'd be afraid it might get back to his wife."

"Well, if you can't drag anything out of your memory, I think I'm going to have to put a little pressure on Mr. Lang," I told him.

He touched my arm and we stopped.

"Don't start pushing my people around, Adams," he warned me.

"I'm not going to push him, Sheriff. In fact, you can come with me to talk to him, if you like. I'll just make my questions a little more direct, that's all."

"Maybe I will tag along with you," he said, taking his hand off my arm so we could start walking again. "It might make him talk a little more freely."

"Like I said before, Sheriff," I said as we reached the hotel, "I'd appreciate any help you could give me."

He nodded, and as I started into the hotel Red followed me.

"You going to take that dog upstairs with you?" Case asked.

I turned to face him, then looked at Red, who was also looking at the Sheriff.

"You tell him he can't come, Sheriff," I told him.

Case looked at Red, who was licking his chops, and said, "Hell, no," and walked away.

"Night, Sheriff." To Red I said, "Say good night to the nice Sheriff, Red."

He woofed once, softly—only the second time I'd heard him make that sound since we hooked up—and we went inside.

10

I didn't have much time to relax the following day, because things happened right off.

As Red and I left the hotel to get some breakfast, I saw the kid, Franklin, standing across the street. I actually saw him before he saw me, and he had probably been waiting for a while. He started in surprise, then stepped down from the walk and crossed the street.

"What a way to start a day," I commended to Red.

Franklin stopped a dozen feet from me and Red began to growl at him. The kid took his eyes off me to look at Red and I could have had him for breakfast, but that wasn't what I was after.

"Quiet, Red," I snapped, and he obeyed.

"I hear you're looking for me," Franklin said.

"Where do you hear that?" I asked.

"I figured I'd save you the trouble," he went on, as if I hadn't spoken. "I'm not going to run from you, Adams, even if I know who you are, now."

"That's admirable, kid, but why do you think I'm looking for you?"

"Somebody took a shot at you last night, and I hear you think it was me."

"Well, I don't know where you heard all these things, but for your information, I know it wasn't you who shot at me last night, so how about that?"

"What the hell are you talking about?"

"You're good with those guns, aren't you?" I asked.

He backed off a bit, saying, "I'm pretty good, yeah. So what?"

"Even in the dark, Franklin, with some lamplight, would you miss me from across the street?"

"Hell, no. I can hit—" he started to brag, the bravado coming back.

"Save it," I told him, and he stopped. "The guy who fired at me last night fired twice, and missed twice. If you wanted to hit me, you wouldn't have missed twice."

He thought it over a moment.

"But Case said—" he began, but then stopped short.

"Yes, Franklin?" I prodded. "Case said what?"

"I only meant—"

"Did Sheriff Case come out to your ranch last night?" I asked.

"Uh, yes."

"And he told your father that I was after you for taking a couple of shots at me?"

"Yes."

"And let me get this right now. Either Case or your father told you that you had to face me down before I could come looking for you."

"Case did. My father wanted me to hide."

So Case had sent this kid after me, knowing full well that he would probably end up dead. That gave me a good idea who had taken those shots at me last night, but I still didn't know why.

Or did I?

"Look, kid, why don't you relax your hands before they cramp. We're not going to be drawing on each other today," I told him.

I walked away, leaving a very puzzled kid behind me. The only thing I'd been doing since I hit town was asking questions about Jenny Sand. Nobody who lived here ten years ago seemed to remember her, and believe me, the way Jenny looked, someone would remember her. The reaction I'd gotten from Lang was convincing me more and more that he remembered her, but something else I was becoming convinced of was that I was getting the runaround from Sheriff Jim Case.

And he was going to explain.

When I got to his office I walked right in, surprising him behind his desk. His hand started to go for his gun, but he hadn't even touched it when I had mine trained on him. It had happened quick because I knew I wasn't going to kill him. Dead, he wouldn't be able to explain.

"Are you crazy?" he asked, half-crouched behind his desk.

"No, I'm just angry. I want to know why you took two shots at me last night, and why you set me up to kill that kid."

"What kid?"

"Franklin."

"You killed Franklin?"

I lost my temper and fired one shot, striking the storm lamp on his desk and sending it careening to the floor. I'll give him this, he didn't flinch.

"Don't play word games with me, Case. You're the second crooked lawman I've run into in two towns, and I don't like it."

He stood up straight, shaking with rage.

"I am not a crooked lawman, Adams. I'm just as much a lawman as you ever were!" he snapped.

Red began to growl as Case's voice rose.

"Not when you send a kid up against me to be killed, you ain't," I told him.

"I wasn't going to let you kill him. Besides, you said yourself, you wouldn't have killed him unless he was especially fast, and he ain't."

"Okay, forget that. Why shoot at me, Case?"

He stared at me a moment, then sat down behind his desk and told me, "You can put up the gun, Adams. You won't need it."

The way he said it made me believe him—and I knew I could get my gun out before him anyway.

"Okay," I said, holstering my gun. "Go ahead."

"I've been waiting ten years for you to show up looking for that girl, Adams," he told me, running his big hand over his face, distorting his features for just a moment.

"You've been waiting for me?"

"I'm supposed to make sure you go in the wrong direction," he explained.

"I don't get this," I told him, shaking my head to clear the fuzziness he was causing. "I suppose that means you know what the right direction is?"

"Yeah, I do."

"And you're supposed to send me the other way?"

"Right."

"Case, that was ten years ago," I reminded him.

"It doesn't matter," he told me. "The man I'm working for has a long memory."

"Yeah, but ten years."

Case just shrugged and said, "This is the way he wanted it."

I decided I had to sit down.

"Adams, this is the only blot on my record. I've been a good lawman. I *am* a good lawman—"

"Okay, Case, I believe you. Look, just tell me where Jenny Sand went when she left here, and who doesn't want me to find her."

He looked like he might, and then he hesitated.

"Look, Case, I'm sure Mr. Franklin would like to know that you sent his kid after me, knowing that he was no match—"

"Wait a minute, Adams, wait a minute," he said, holding up his hands. "I'm caught in the middle here, you understand?"

"No, I don't understand."

"All right, look, I'll make a deal with you. I'll tell you where she went, but you can't say you heard it from me."

"And?"

Shaking his head he said, "I can't tell you who I got my instructions from. Even threatening me with Franklin won't get me to tell you that, because one's as bad as the other."

Since the big question was where Jenny went when she left Red Sky, I decided to settle for his deal. I could find out the rest when I found her.

"Okay, Case. Agreed."

He looked relieved to some degree.

"Okay, then," he said.

"Case," I said, before he could go on, "if you lie to me, I'll come back for you."

"I'm not going to lie to you. She took the stage, ten years ago, to Mexico."

Mexico. That was a long trip, and through Comanche country, too.

"Did you get the word on me right away?" I asked.

"Uh, no, it was a few months after she left. That's all I can say, Adams—except that when you get to Mexico, be careful."

"Mexico's a big place, Case. C'mon, give me all of it."

He put his hand over his mouth, then took it away. He was chewing on his lips.

"All right, okay. She went to a town called—uh, I can't say it in Spanish, but it means 'blessed gate.'"

"Blessed Gate," I repeated. I didn't know how to say it in Spanish, but I'd find out along the way.

I got up and headed for the door.

"Adams, uh, is that it?"

"That's all I wanted, Case. You can wrestle with your conscience about what you did. If you're the lawman you think you are, I'm sure you have one."

I left him contemplating that, not wondering in the least what would happen to him after I left.

I was looking ahead, and I didn't care what I left behind.

I went right to the livery and told the man to get Duke and my rig ready to roll. I checked out of the hotel—to the delight of the management—and paid my bill. The clerk kept his eyes on Red the whole time, because Red was teasing him, growling and baring his teeth. I bared my teeth at him myself for a couple of seconds just before we walked out.

"Animals," I heard him mutter as we left. I looked down at Red, and it didn't seem to bother him, so I didn't let it bother me.

11

I stopped at the next town to put up my rig. I didn't
want to get caught in the heart of Comanche country,
and be unable to move fast. To move fast all I needed
was Duke. Red decided to tag along with us, but if it
came down to it, he would be on his own.

I was able to avoid contact with Comanches most of
the way, until I was a couple of days from the Mexican
border. I saw them coming, and ducked out of sight with
Duke and Red. I would have avoided them all together
but they had a white woman with them. Once I realized
that, I had to change my direction and trail along until
I could figure some way of rescuing her.

I was lucky in one respect; there were only half a
dozen of them. It could have been worse. I'd been hiding
from parties with twelve to twenty braves. However,
whether there were six, twelve or twenty of them, there
was still only one of me, and getting her away from them
wouldn't be easy.

After a day of trailing them, I decided that I had to do
something, because they were taking me too far from my
intended destination. There was only one thing to do. I
had to wait for the moment when they were relaxed and
unaware, and then ride in on them with my rifle and my
revolver blasting. With luck, I'd take care of them all

before they recovered. If there had been more of them, I never would have tried it. Also, from what I could see, only three of them had rifles, and the other three bows and arrows. I'd have to take the three riflemen out first.

As it turned out, my only opportunity was that night, when they camped. The darkness was my only ally. It would take them some time to see me. By then, half of them would be dead.

Then again, they were Comanches. For all I knew, they were waiting for me.

I never got a good look at the girl. I saw only that she was dark-haired. She also appeared young; the fact that the Comanches had bothered to grab her supported that observation. If she had been old, the Comanches would either have killed her or left her where they found her.

I decided to stop thinking and start doing, because thinking might make me change my mind. All doing could do was get me killed.

With any other horse I might have had to try riding in with the reins in my teeth, while I fired my guns with either hand, but with Duke I simply had to show him where I wanted to go. He didn't like it, but we had agreed long ago that I was the ramrod of our outfit, and we went where I said.

"Okay, big boy," I said. "We're almost ready."

I took out my rifle and held it on one hand, and grasped my revolver in the other. I'd only be able to squeeze off one shot at a time with the rifle, and maybe only one shot, period, but it was a different story with my revolver. I had modified the gun myself, converting it to double-action. That meant that I didn't have to cock the hammer before I fired, all I had to do was pull the trigger. Double-action guns were not then common; I had gotten the idea from reading about an Englishman named Adams.

If I'd thought of it, I might have taken a second hand-

gun out of my rig before I left it behind, but that was
neither here nor there. I had six shots in my handgun,
and I planned on making every one count. The rifle was
insurance.

"Okay, big boy," I told Duke when I was ready, "let's
get it over with."

Duke took off and I gripped him with my knees. As
we approached the campfire, the six men and one woman all looked up, the same shocked expression on all
their faces. I wiped it off one face with my first shot. One
of the rifleman went for his gun, but I caught him before
he reached it and he went down also. We swept on
through the camp and I circled Duke around to come
through a second time.

One man had gotten his hands on his rifle and was
bringing it to bear on me when a red blur smacked into
him.

That mongrel dog again!

The second time through I squeezed off three quick
shots, and three of the braves went spinning to the
ground. Unfortunately, one of the bowman got off a
shaft, and I felt the shock of pain and numbness as it hit
me in the shoulder. I stayed on Duke's back long
enough to make sure that the brave Red was struggling
with was dead, and then I fell off the big black, and just
kept on falling.

12

I never felt myself land, but land I did, because when I came around I was on my back. My head was lying on something soft and warm, and above me was the face of a very pretty little lady. She had big brown eyes, a strong, straight nose and a full-lipped mouth. She was a lovely thing to wake up to.

"Well, at least it was worth it," I said.

"What?" she asked.

"Nothing."

"Mister, are you going to stay awake this time?" she asked me.

"Why, have I been awake before?" I asked.

"Yes, but you never spoke."

"Then I guess I'm awake for good, this time."

I got the feeling she was even more frightened than she was letting on.

"The arrow," I said, feeling for my shoulder.

"Don't touch," she warned me, grabbing my hand. "I think it hit a bone, because it didn't go in very deep. I pulled it out and patched you up as best I could."

"Thanks."

"I should be thanking you. Those savages have been dragging me around for days. I can just imagine what they were going to do to me when we got to wherever we were going."

"No," I told her. "I don't think you can."

She frowned. "Are you delirious?" she asked.

"No, I'm not. Help me sit up, will you?"

"Do you think you should?"

"I think I'd better," I told her. She put her hands behind my back and helped me to a seated position. "It doesn't feel too bad," I told her. "We'll probably be able to move out in the morning."

"Thank God for that," she said, looking around. I did the same and found that we were sitting right in the midst of the six dead Indians.

"All these bodies," she said, shuddering, "and that crazy dog of yours," she added, pointing to where Red was sitting, watching us. "He won't even let me touch him."

"He's not mine," I told her. "He just follows me around."

"Well, he sure tore into that Indian when he pointed his gun at you," she remarked, indicating the Indian with the bullet hole in his head, and half his hand torn off.

"Once in a while he makes himself useful," I admitted. I looked around and spotted Duke, standing behind us. Red was in front of us, and Duke behind. Those damned animals were working together.

"Hiya, big boy," I called out, and he whinnied in return.

"These two animals are almost human," she remarked.

"And I'm just enough animal for the three of us to get along," I added. She looked at me oddly, but I didn't give her a chance to speak.

"I think you'd better get some rest," I told her. She was too calm for me. I thought she might even be in shock. "Get some sleep."

"Here?" she asked, waving her arms around, indicating the bodies around us.

"Move over there," I told her, waving my own hand at the darkness around us.

She looked out there, as if considering it, then said, "No thanks," and moved closer to me. "Just let me stay close to you, all right?"

"Sure, but I'm going to sleep, too."

"Well, who's going to stand guard?"

"They are," I said, pointing to Red and Duke.

She stared at me, trying to figure out if I was serious or not, then said, "This is crazy, but why the hell not. Nothing's been normal since those savages grabbed me. I was—"

"We'll talk about it in the morning," I told her. "C'mon, get some sleep. You need it."

Suddenly her eyes got very heavy and she said, "You know, this is actually the safest I've felt in days. You're right, I am tired."

She put her head against my good shoulder and we lay like that, together. I was aware that she had a nice body beneath the blanket that had been thrown over her. I also became aware that she wasn't wearing anything beneath the blanket. Even with the pain in my shoulder, I could feel the stirring in my loins as she tried to make herself comfortable against me.

"My name's Angel," she murmured even after I thought she was asleep. "It's short for Angelique."

"That's a pretty name," I told her. "Mine's Clint."

"Thank you very much, Clint. I'm going to sleep now."

"Good, so am I."

And we did.

13

I woke first the next morning and was surprised to find only a twinge of pain in my shoulder. I nudged Angelique gently because I wanted to get an early start. We were at least three days from the border, and I wanted to try to cut it to two. I also wanted to find a water hole where I could bathe my wounded shoulder.

"What—where—" she stammered as she woke up, trying to get her bearings.

"Easy, Angel, easy. Everything's all right now," I reminded her.

She looked around wide-eyed for a few more seconds, then it dawned on her that her situation had changed and she seemed to relax some.

"How do you feel?" I asked her.

"Fine, I feel fine—and the sooner we can get away from here, I'll feel even better."

"Well then, help me to my feet and let's get going."

She helped me up and I discovered that there wasn't as little pain as I had thought.

"Listen, Angel, grab one of those ponies. You're going to need one of them."

She turned and looked around. They had scattered during the shooting, but during the night they had wandered back to the fire, and one or two of them were within easy reach.

"No problem," she assured me.

I watched as she approached one of the ponies, speaking to it in low tones, soothing it so it wouldn't bolt. I was impressed with the way she handled the animal. Apparently, she'd spent a lot of time around horses.

I called Duke over and he helped me mount by going down to his front knees.

"I don't believe that," Angel said, riding alongside us on the pony.

"That's one of his easier tricks," I assured her.

"He doesn't have to do any tricks," she told me, patting his neck. "He's absolutely gorgeous. You wouldn't want to sell him, would you?"

"Sell Duke?" I asked. "I don't think that's possible. We kind of belong to each other, you know?"

"I think so," she said, but I wasn't convinced she was satisfied with the answer. "Should we get going?" she asked.

"In a minute."

Apparently she had replaced my gun in my holster, because I hadn't had to look for it on the ground. My rifle was also in the scabbard on my saddle. I took them both out now and reloaded them. We were still in Comanche country, with a long way to go.

"Do you think anyone heard the shooting?" she asked.

"It's possible," I said, replacing the rifle in its scabbard, "but we're getting an early start. Comanches would wait until morning to come and investigate, anyway."

I put my gun back in my holster, then said, "We might as well get started. I want to make Mexico as quickly as possible."

"Good, that's where I live," she told me.

I thought I had detected some kind of an accent in her speech, but I hadn't been able to identify it.

As we started riding I asked, "Are you Mexican?"

"My father is. My mother was French. I only spoke Spanish and French until I was ten, then I learned English."

"You speak it very well," I complimented her.

"Thank you."

We did a lot of talking while we rode, mostly because I was trying to keep her mind off what had happened. Oddly enough, though, that was mostly what we talked about.

She'd been out riding on her father's ranch, and had exceeded the boundaries of his land. Before she knew what had happened, she was surrounded by the six Comanches, who dragged her off her horse, and deposited her on a pony.

"Odd that it was Comanches who grabbed you," I remarked, "and not Apaches."

Years ago, the Apaches had lived in Texas, but eventually the more ferocious Comanches had forced them across the border into Mexico. Since then there had been occasional raiding parties of Apaches into Texas, but rarely did it work the other way.

"Well, if you say they were Comanches, I will take your word for it," she told me. "All I knew was that they were Indians."

She went on to tell me that her father owned one of the largest ranches in all of Mexico.

"Where is it located?" I asked.

"I will tell you in English," she told me. "It is just outside a town called Blessed Gate."

"Really?"

"Have you heard of the town?" she asked.

"It seems to me I've heard the name," I replied. I decided against telling her that was where I headed.

"And why are you going to Mexico, Señor Adams?"

"Clint, please," I told her. I stretched the truth some

by answering, "I'm supposed to meet a friend there."

There was a lull in the conversation and I could see a pensive look cross her face. I was afraid she'd start thinking back, so I started looking for things to talk about.

"How old are you?" I asked.

She snapped her head in my direction, and for a moment I thought she didn't hear the question.

"I am nineteen."

"Do you have any other nicknames?" I asked.

"You do not like 'Angel'?"

"I like Angelique a whole lot better," I admitted.

"It is much too long. I do have another nickname," she admitted, "one which I prefer."

"What's that?"

"Angie."

"Angie," I repeated. I liked it.

"May I call you 'Angie'?" I asked.

"You have earned the right."

"Thank you."

Eventually we ran out of talk, and rode in silence. The conversation had served to take my mind off my injury; now I was aware again of the throbbing pain. I was concerned about possible infection, which is why I wanted to find water before long. As yet there was no burning sensation and it didn't seem to be too sensitive, so I wasn't overly worried at the moment. Still, I would have liked to bathe it as soon as possible. I had water in my canteen, but it had to last the two of us.

"How is your shoulder?" she asked.

"It'll be okay," I assured her.

"You need a doctor to look at it," she said.

"It should be all right."

"I hope so. It is my fault that you were injured."

"That's silly," I told her.

After that we both got all talked out and it wasn't

until darkness began to approach that we conversed again.

"Will we be stopping soon?" she asked.

"I just want to cover as much ground as possible before—" I began, but then I stopped short and reined Duke in.

"What's wrong?" she asked, stopping a few steps ahead of us.

"I smell something," I told her, sniffing at the air. I turned my head left and right.

"Smoke," I said. "I smell smoke . . . and something cooking."

She lifted her nose as high as she could and sniffed the air herself.

"I don't—wait, yes I do. I smell it. Where is it coming from?" she asked. "Is it a campfire?" she asked.

I shook my head, still searching for the direction. "I don't think so," I said slowly, and then saw it. If it had been a shade darker I would have missed it, but there it was, a thin column of dark smoke, as if it were coming from a chimney.

"Follow me," I told her, kicking Duke into action.

When it got darker I was traveling on memory and instinct, because I could no longer see the column.

"Where are we going?" she demanded after a while.

"There," I said, pointing. It had just come into view, after we topped a rise.

"A house," she breathed in surprise.

"That's right. We can get some help there." If we didn't get shot riding in. A lone house in the middle of Comanche country wouldn't habitually receive visitors.

"Listen, when we get close enough, you sing out," I told her. "They might react more favorably to a woman's voice than to a man's."

"All right."

"If someone comes out, tell them the truth, the whole

story. I can't think of a lie that would go over better."

"All right," she said again.

When we were getting within shouting distance, someone beat her to it. There was a shot and a spurt of dirt in front of Duke. He stood his ground, but the pony shied a bit.

"Hold him," I told her.

"I have him," she assured me.

"What do you want?" a masculine voice called out from the house.

"Go ahead," I urged her.

"We need help," she called out.

"Who's with you?" the voice called.

"A man. He saved me from the Comanches and was wounded. He needs help."

No answer.

"Please," she cried out, a little louder. There must have been just the right touch of panic and girlishness in her voice, because the voice called out, "Come in a little closer."

She rode in closer, so he could make out who we were. He stood in the doorway until he was sure we weren't Comanches, then stepped out, holding an old Henry on us. A woman stood behind him, looking frightened, but her expression changed when she saw Angie.

"Land sakes," she cried out, "look at that pore chile," and ran over to Angie's horse.

"Mama, come back here," the man shouted, but she disregarded him. They both appeared to be in their fifties, sturdily-built people used to making their way out here.

"Mister, I could use a hand," I told him.

He stepped closer, saw the blood on my shirt, then made his decision. He set the rifle down on the steps, then came to help me off Duke. His wife was chattering about bloody savages, and Angie was explaining her predicament, and how I helped her out of it. The man kept silent while he assisted me inside.

Eventually, the woman got around to my shoulder, and she got a bath ready for Angie in the other room.

"I'll go out and tend to the horses," the man finally spoke, "while Mama tends your wound."

He had some kind of an accent, that I'd heard somewhere before. Swedish, I think it was.

"Take good care of my black, will you? He's special."

"I could see that when you rode in," he assured me.

"Papa knows horses," the woman told me while she cleaned my shoulder. She used the last of a bottle of whisky to clean it.

"Any infection?" I asked.

"Not that I can see," she said. "This must have hurt plenty."

"Yeah, it stung some," I admitted.

"That little girl is lucky you came along," she went on. She kept up a steady stream of chatter while she bandaged me.

The old man came back in and went straight to a cupboard, took out a bottle of whisky and handed it to me without a glass.

"Thank you," I said, accepting the full bottle.

At that point, Angie came in, looking clean and fresh in a yellow dress.

"That was my daughter's," the woman said. "She was almost as pretty as you are, my dear."

"Thank you," Angie said.

Actually pretty was an understatement, now that I was able to get a good look at her. She had well-rounded breasts, a tiny waist and flaring hips. The blanket she had been wearing had well disguised her charms, but they were obvious now, and I was impressed.

"Is he all right?" she asked the woman.

"Don't you worry, he will be fine."

We all exchanged names. They were Mr. and Mrs. Linquist, and they'd lived in that house for eleven years.

"Papa built it himself," she said proudly.

"Have you had much trouble with Comanches?" I asked him.

He shook his head solemnly.

"They leave us alone and we leave them alone."

You couldn't predict what the Comanches would do. For some reason they had chosen to allow the Linquists to live there in peace.

"You will move on in the morning," Linquist said, making it more of a statement than a question.

"Papa!" his wife scolded, but he kept looking at me.

"Yes, Mr. Linquist, we'll move on," I assured him.

He nodded.

"You must both be hungry," Mrs. Linquist said. "I will get you some stew."

She came back with two bowls teeming with meat, potatoes, and chunks of bread. I washed it down with the Linquists' whisky.

After dinner Linquist said, "We will sleep out here. The girl can sleep inside with Mama," he told us.

"Yah, of course," Mama agreed. "You come, child. You need your rest after your ordeal."

Angie looked at me and said, "Good night, Clint."

"Good night, kid. See you bright and early."

She and Mrs. Linquist went into the bedroom, and then Mama reappeared with some blankets for Papa and me.

I took the last couple of hits from the whisky bottle and passed it back to Linquist. He took it, corked it, and returned it to the cupboard. He doused the light, plunging us into darkness.

"You have a beautiful horse," he said from the dark.

"Thanks," I said, caught off balance by the remark.

"Is the dog yours?" he asked.

Damn, I'd forgotten about Red.

"Where is he?" I asked.

"Right outside the door."

I started to sit up, saying, "I've got to give him something—"

"Momma gave him some stew," he told me.

I stopped.

"I hope she didn't try to touch him."

"She simply fed him."

That was a relief. All I needed was for Red to bite the hand that had fed us.

14

The next morning I asked Mrs. Linquist if she'd give
Red some eggs, just to make up for my forgetting him
the night before.

"Eggs for the dog?" she asked, looking at me like I
was crazy. She shrugged. "If that's what you want."

"Thank you."

While she was at it, she made some for Angie too,
who wolfed it down. I settled for coffee and some
biscuits, and then we were ready to leave.

Mrs. Linquist had given Angie some riding clothes
which had also belonged to her daughter, and then we
were on our way.

Angie was quiet for a long time before asking, "Did
you and Mr. Linquist talk?"

"Nope. That man doesn't say anymore than he has
to."

"He's bitter."

"About what?"

"Their daughter. She was killed."

I looked at her.

"By Comanches?"

"By one Indian. Mr. Linquist tracked him down and
killed him. After that the Comanches did not bother
them."

Linquist didn't look like he could kill a Comanche warrior, but I guess you can't tell from looks. By some strange code, I guess the Comanches figured they owed the Linquists something for the death of their daughter.

"I guess the man's got reason to be bitter," I said. "What about Mrs. Linquist?"

"I think that nice lady is mad."

There had been a kind of glassy look to her eyes, I remembered. Could it be that we had left a bitter old man and a crazy old lady behind in that house?

I decided not to think about it anymore. Madness could have been just the reason that the superstitious Comanches did not go near the Linquist house.

"How sad," Angie said.

"Don't think about it," I told her. "Just don't think about it."

MEXICO
1871

15

Since both horses were well rested and well fed, I pushed them, and we made the border before dark. In fact, we still had a few hours of daylight left when we crossed into Mexico.

"How far to Blessed Gate?" I asked.

She looked at the sky. "I guess we could make it by nightfall. But how is your shoulder?"

"Fine."

She knew I was lying.

"I suppose it would be better if we pushed on," she remarked, "that way we could have a doctor look at you tonight."

"Good point," I said, wincing as a spasm of pain lanced through my shoulder.

"I suggest we push on," she said, and urged her pony forward.

"Good suggestion," I said to myself, and sent Duke after her.

As the darkness fell, I began to worry less about Comanches and Apaches and about being shot from my saddle. I began to think about something I hadn't had time to think about in days. Jenny.

I thought about the way she looked and felt, the way she smelled, even the way she tasted. All these things I could still remember, even after thirteen years. I wondered how the years might have changed her.

Had she changed as drastically as I had?

I hoped not.

"There it is," Angie said suddenly. I rode up next to her and looked down at the town of Blessed Gate.

The town was a mixture of wooden and adobe structures. It was alive with lights, but there was very little activity in the streets.

"It is a quiet town," she observed, "and the people are good. I hope your friend is there waiting for you." She had put a special emphasis on the word "friend."

"I hope so, too"

She elected to lead the way into town, and I elected to let her.

Once in town she rode right past the livery stable.

"The livery—" I began.

"First the doctor," she said over her shoulder.

I let her have her head, since it was her town.

She pulled up in front of one of the adobe buildings and dismounted.

"I will get someone to help you off your horse," she told me. "Wait there."

She went inside, and in a moment came out with a tall man with gray hair and a pencil-thin mustache. He was in shirt sleeves and was chewing something, so I assumed that we had interrupted his dinner.

"I am Doctor Montoya," he told me.

"Sorry to interrupt your dinner, Doc."

He reached for me to help me down from Duke's back and said, "Don't be concerned about that, my friend. We will get you inside and look you over. My dinner will be waiting."

When my feet hit the ground he steadied me by holding my elbows. Over his shoulder he asked Angie, "You will be coming in, Señorita Angel?"

"No, Miguel. Clint, I will arrange a room for you at the hotel. Miguel will tell you where it is."

"Where are you going?" I asked.

"I will see you tomorrow," she promised. With that she jumped on the pony's back and started off down the street.

"Where is she going?"

"I am more concerned for you, my friend, then with her. Shall we go inside so I may tend your wound?"

Inside I stripped off my shirt and he looked at my wound.

"Whoever cleaned it did an excellent job," he commented, looking closely at it. "There is no sign of infection at all. You were lucky, my friend, and so was the señorita, that you happened along when you did."

"I agree, on both counts," I told him.

"You will be staying in town long?" he asked, looking at my wound from over the top of his glasses.

"I don't know yet. I'm, ah, hoping to meet someone here."

"A friend?"

"An old friend."

"I see."

He put a new bandage on my shoulder and told me, "I don't anticipate any problems with your wound, Señor. You should heal very nicely."

"Thank you, Doctor," I said, standing up and putting my shirt back on for the walk to the hotel. "What do I owe you?"

"There is no charge, Señor," he said, putting his equipment away.

He turned to face me and said, "Your horse has been taken to the livery stable, with instructions for special care."

"Well, thank you for that, too," I said, surprised at the royal treatment I seemed to be getting, and apparently all because of little Angie.

"I can have someone take you to the hotel," he offered.

"Instructions will do nicely," I assured him. "I can find my way."

"Very well." He gave me easy instructions, with only one right turn thrown in.

"And the livery?"

That was the other way, with a left turn.

"Have you seen the dog?"

"The big red one?"

"That's the one."

"I believe he's right outside. Is he yours?"

"He follows me."

"Ah, I see," he said. "I believe I will get back to my dinner now, Señor."

"Of course. Again, I apologize for taking you away from it."

"I assure you, no apology is necessary."

We shook hands and I left his home, which also appeared to serve as his office.

I walked to the hotel with Red at my side, found it to be one of the wooden structures in town.

I approached the clerk and said, "My name is Adams."

"Yes, sir, we have a room waiting for you. Your belongings have already been brought up."

"Thank you."

"Is the dog yours, sir?" the clerk asked.

"He's a friend of mine, yes, but I'm afraid I don't have much control over him. Do you object to his following me upstairs?"

"Oh, no sir, of course not. Please," he said, extending the key to me. "Let us know if there's anything we can get for you."

"A bottle of whisky would be nice," I said.

"Of course, sir, it will be brought up to you," he assured me. He was a dapper little man with slicked down hair who had the habit of bowing his head everytime he called me sir.

"Thank you," I told him, and went up the steps.

When I got to my room I let Red go in ahead of me, then shut the door behind us. He picked a corner and curled up in it.

"Tired, aren't you?" I asked.

He stared at me.

"Won't admit it, huh? Well, I will. I'm bushed. I'm going to have a couple of drinks and get some sleep."

There was a knock at the door and it was a small boy with a bottle of whiskey. I gave him two bits and took the bottle.

"Guess I should have ordered something for you, eh boy?" I asked Red.

He didn't reply.

"Oh, well, we'll get you some eggs in the morning."

Since no glass had been brought with the bottle—a terrible oversight that I'd take up with the manager—I took a couple of stiff nips from the bottle, then stripped off my clothes and fell on the bed.

My last thought was to wonder why I rated red-carpet treatment. Guess I'd find that out tomorrow.

16

Morning came, and brought some stiffness with it, but all things considered, I didn't feel too bad. After a bath and a shave, I felt almost human.

I had two pots of coffee with breakfast, and Red had two helpings of eggs, and I decided that we'd both go down to the livery stable and see how Duke was doing. After that I planned on going through the town, trying to find someone who knew Jenny.

"How you doing, big boy?" I asked, as the livery man took me to Duke's stall.

"He is a beautiful animal, Señor," the man told me. "I have been taking very special care of him." He seemed especially proud of the job he'd been doing since last night.

Duke looked like he'd been brushed and well fed, and he nuzzled my hand to indicate that he was glad to see me.

"Yeah, I'm glad to see you, too," I said, patting his neck.

"He has a name?" the Mexican asked.

"Duke."

"Duke? That is a name for a beautiful horse?" he asked, looking puzzled.

"It's the one he answers to," I assured him. "What's your name?"

"Tico."

"Well, Tico, you keep taking good care of Duke the way you have been, and I'll be very grateful, eh?" I said, pressing some dollars into his hand.

"Si Señor, gracias," he said, stuffing the money into his pockets. He turned back to Duke and started talking in Spanish, either to himself or Duke. I hoped he was talking to himself, because Duke wouldn't understand a word he was saying.

"Okay, Red, time to go looking for our 'friend,' " I told the big red mongrel.

I started in the general store, asking if there was anyone working there now who worked there ten years ago. I didn't go straight to the sheriff's office because I'd had bad experiences the last two times I did that. It bothered me, having second thoughts about going to the local law for help, but there it was. It had to be somebody big involved, to make a man like Jim Case keep a promise ten years after he made it. I'd go to the law in Blessed Gate in due time, but first I'd make the rounds of the town and see what I could dig up.

I drew a blank at the general store, not so much on information as with a language barrier. Funny thing was, we were communicating okay until I mentioned Jenny's name, then the clerk behind the counter suddenly had a problem saying anything but "No speak English."

Somebody had exerted a lot of pressure, from Mexico to Texas, and the door was shut tight. I tried a few more stores in town, and came up with the same answer.

The saloon—or cantina, if you like—was next.

"Beer," I told the bartender, and then remembering one of the only Spanish words I knew, I said, "Cerveca," which is Spanish for beer.

"Cerveca," he repeated, putting it down in front of me.

"Gracias."

For some reason, Red had chose to enter the cantina with me, something he hadn't done since we first hooked up together.

"He is yours?" the bartender asked.

I looked down and found Red sitting at my feet.

"Actually, he just kind of follows me around," I told him.

"Take him out," he said, frowning. Apparently, he was not a dog-lover. He was also about twice my girth, although he was barely an inch or so taller. He was built along the lines of a bull.

"I can't," I told him.

"Take him out," he repeated.

"He'll bite me," I said.

He stared at me a moment, then leaned over and looked at Red again.

"Vamanos!" he shouted, but it had no effect on Red.

"He doesn't understand Spanish," I warned him.

Muttering to himself he started around the bar, obviously intent on physically kicking Red out of the cantina. Gratefully, I never found out if he could, because as he came around another voice called out, "Ernesto!"

The bartender straightened up at the sound of his name and looked around. It was the Doctor, Miguel Montoya, who had just entered the cantina.

"Momentito," the doctor said, approaching the big man. He spoke into the bartender's ear, and the larger man's face changed as he listened. When the doctor was finished speaking, Ernesto had apparently forgotten his previous intention, and he went back behind the bar.

The doctor approached me and I asked, "What did you tell him that took the fire out of his eyes?"

"I told him that you were a special friend, and that this made your animal very special, as well. May I join you?"

"Please."

"Shall we take a table?"

"Lead the way."

He made a hand signal, which the big bartender seemed to understand, and led me to a corner table. I sat with my back to the wall. Ernesto brought over a glass of what looked like brandy for the doctor, and retreated.

"I don't think he likes me," I commented.

"Oh, Ernest frowns at everyone. Do not let it concern you." He sipped his brandy and then asked, "How goes your search for your friend?" There was too much effort to make the question sound innocent.

With the amount of pressure—from here to Texas, remember—I figured that someone would approach me sooner or later. All I had to do was keep asking questions.

"Not very well, I'm afraid. It seems that no one in town has ever heard of her. Or is willing to admit to it."

"I see. Then your friend is a woman."

"Yes, she is."

"What is her name. Perhaps I know her."

"I'm sure you know her name, Doctor. I'm sure you've been made aware of the fact that I've been asking questions around town."

He sipped his brandy, not replying to my statement.

"All right, Doctor, play it your way. Her name was Jenny Sand when I knew her, thirteen years ago. For all I know, her name could be different, now, but whatever her name is, the trail has led here and I'd like to see her."

I drained my beer and stood up. Red jumped to his feet, as if sensing how tense I was.

"You tell that to whoever sent you here, huh Doc?" I told him. "You tell them I'd like to see her. It's been a long time."

"How is your shoulder?" he asked, trying to throw me off balance.

"It's fine, Doc. You're a good doctor—I just hope you're as good a messenger boy."

17

I stepped outside and made a conscious effort to force the tension out of my body. When I had successfully done that, I decided that more questions would be fruitless under the circumstances. Instead I would observe a Mexican custom and take a siesta. I claimed an empty chair in front of my hotel. I needed the rest. Angling the chair against the building, and putting my feet up against a post, I tipped my hat down over my eyes and told Red, "Don't let anyone take my gun."

He looked up at me, yawned, and lowered himself to the ground, as if to say, Look out for yourself, pal.

"Thanks."

It seemed I had just drifted off when a big hand prodded my shoulder—my wounded shoulder, which is why it didn't take a whole lot of prodding to get my attention.

"Shit!" I snapped, bringing the chair back to all four legs with a bang. I grabbed my shoulder and looked up to see who wanted my attention.

The first thing I saw was the big star on his chest, and then I looked behind it. The sheriff was not very tall, but sturdy-looking, with an old Navy colt on his right hip. He was also an American.

"How come you ain't a Mex?" I asked.

"Blame my parents," he told me. "I'd like you to come over to my office with me, Adams. If you've got the time." He had a deep bass voice, which seemed to rumble around in his barrel chest before it eventually found its way out.

"Well," I said, massaging my shoulder. "I was kind of busy."

"That a bad shoulder?" he asked. "Sorry about that."

"It's okay," I told him. "No harm done, I don't think." I stood up and said, "Let's go over to your office."

"That your dog?" he asked.

Red had his advantages, but I was sure tired of hearing that question.

"Why?"

"Don't much like dogs."

"I wouldn't tell him that if I were you," I warned him.

He looked at Red, who just stared back, then shrugged and said, "This way."

He started off down the street, then looked behind him, either to see if I was following, or if Red was. We both were, so he just turned his head back and kept walking.

His office was an adobe building with a heavy, oak door. He opened it and went in ahead of me. I followed, and Red chose to wait outside. The sheriff seemed to appreciate that fact when I shut the door behind me and took a seat in front of his desk.

"What's this about, Sheriff?"

He took off his hat and placed it on his desk. His hair was gray and cut short, but he ran his hand through it anyway.

"Well, you're a visitor to our town, Mr. Adams," he told me. "I like to make the acquaintance of all strangers who come to town."

"Well," I began, pushing myself to my feet, "if that's all, then we've done it—"

"Sit down, Mr. Adams," he snapped, then added, "please."

I lowered myself back into the chair, folded my hands across my stomach, and waited.

He scratched his nose for a few seconds, out of habit, I suspected, not need. He seemed to be wondering where to start, and I decided to be patient and wait him out.

"You've been asking a lot of questions around town, Mr. Adams," he finally said.

"Uh-huh."

"Trying to locate a friend, I understand."

"An old friend."

He nodded.

He looked up at the ceiling and said, "Well, it seems like your questions have upset a few people."

"I can't understand why," I told him.

"Well, to tell you the truth, neither can I," he admitted, scratching his ear, now, "but I've gotten a few complaints, and I got to do my job."

"I understand that."

"I guess you would," he commented. "You were a lawman for a long time yourself, weren't you?"

"I didn't think my rep would travel this far," I told him.

"Oh, I've heard of you, all right," he assured me. "You've got a rep as a lawman, but you've also got a rep with a gun. You wouldn't be here to use that gun, would you?"

"No, I wouldn't."

He nodded again.

"Okay, here's the way it goes, Mr. Adams. I'd ask you to leave town, but you did yourself a big favor by bringing Angelique Soto back safe and sound. Her pappy should be very grateful. He's a big man in these parts. In fact, he's a big man in any parts."

An idea dawned on me then.

"Texas?"

He nodded.

"Texas, Oklahoma, Missouri, you name it, he's got connections."

The idea began to blossom.

"Anyway, I'm not gonna ask you to leave, but I am gonna ask you to stop asking questions."

That seemed reasonable to agree to, since I'd already decided to stop, anyway.

"Okay, and I'll ask you to do something."

"What's that?"

"Talk to Doctor Montoya. He may have something important to tell you," I said, getting up from my chair.

"Is that a fact?" he asked, getting up and walking to the door with me.

"And what might that be?"

I walked outside and Red got up and stood next to me. I turned back to the sheriff and told him, "He just might tell you that I'm a very special person."

18

I had the impression that the sheriff—whose name I hadn't thought to ask—didn't know whatever Dr. Montoya knew. I also had the feeling that, before long, he would.

Now I knew something now I hadn't known before. Angie's last name was Soto, and her father was a big man, both in the U.S. and Mexico. However, as big as he apparently was, I had never heard of him.

Was he the man trying to keep me from finding Jenny? And if so, why?

The best thing I could do was hang around, and not ask anymore questions. I decided to do some drinking, some card-playing, and some heavy waiting.

I went over to the cantina and appropriated a deck of cards and a corner table. With my back to the wall, and Red at my feet, I played solitaire until some likely prospects walked in. Three of them; two Mexicans, and one American.

For some reason the American caught my eye. He was about thirty, slim, not tall, with a dark black mustache and dark eyes. He wore a Colt on his right hip, and he wore it low. The two Mexicans with him also wore guns, but theirs were high on their waist. They were just ranch hands, and their guns were just something to wear, like their hats and their boots. The American was a different story.

"Poker?" I asked them when my shuffling caught their attention.

They looked at each other, and all agreed. As the evening wore on, we gained a fifth player.

"You three work together?" I asked.

"Si," one of the Mexicans answered. "We work for Señor Soto, at Rancho Soto. Biggest spread in all of Mexico."

"Is that right?" I asked, trying to sound impressed. The Mexicans didn't mind talking, but the American was a quiet one. All I found out about him was his name, which didn't mean anything to me. It was Bags, Joe Bags.

The fifth player was someone who lived in town, and I wasn't interested in him at all.

The only decent poker player of the lot was Bags, so it very often came down to the two of us, and we seemed to be splitting the pots fifty-fifty.

"Look like we're evenly matched," he said in a rare moment when he spoke more than two words.

"Seems that way," I agreed.

When we called the game, most of the money was evenly piled in front of me and Joe Bags. The two Mexican hands stood up, muttering in Spanish, while the Mexican from town just shook his head and walked out.

"We are going back to the ranch," one Mexican told Joe Bags.

"I'll be along in a while," he told them. They shrugged and left without him.

When they were gone he said, "I wonder if they think they were taken by a couple of American sharpies."

"You're a good card player," I told him.

"So are you. You're Clint Adams, aren't you?" he asked.

"That's right."

"I thought I recognized you," he said.

"I don't know you, do I?" I asked, studying his face again.

He shook his head.

"No, you wouldn't. I saw you and Wild Bill stand off eight men a few years back. Shit, where the hell was that?" he asked himself. "I can't remember where, but I remember the incident," he assured me.

"Yeah, well, that's happened once or twice, so I couldn't tell which time you're talking about, but I'm glad you enjoyed it."

"Ho, I did that," he said, and for a moment he looked younger than I'd originally tagged him.

I held my hand up for the bartender to see, and then made signs to indicate I wanted a bottle and two glasses.

"What should we drink to?" I asked when we each had a drink in hand.

He shrugged.

"Who needs the excuse to drink?" he asked.

I agreed with him, and we drank.

"How long you been working out at Rancho Soto?" I asked him.

"Just a few months. I wandered into Mexico with a bunch of Apaches on my tail. Some of the riders from the ranch helped me out. The foreman offered me a job, and I stayed on."

"Pay good?" I asked.

"Real good," he answered, and downed another drink. "You looking for a job?"

I shook my head.

"No, I work for myself now."

"Not a lawman anymore?" he asked.

"No."

"I thought maybe you were tracking somebody," he remarked. I looked closer at him, but his remark appeared innocent enough.

"I am, but there's no price involved. I hear Soto's got a good-looking daughter."

"And how," he said, and his eyes brightened. It looked like Bags had it bad for the boss's daughter. "She got herself in a jam a couple of days back—well, more than that. Indians grabbed her while she was riding, but she's back now. Somebody got her back, I heard—" and then he stopped because a thought had apparently struck him. "Say, you wouldn't know anything about that, would you?"

"I guess I would, Joe," I admitted.

"Hey, old man Soto's liable to be very grateful to you," he told me.

"You get along with the old guy?"

"Hell, ain't hardly seen him but once or twice in all the months I'm working there. I'm just a hand."

We had a few more drinks, and then he said it was time for him to be getting back.

"Thanks for the drinks, and the game," he said, standing up.

"Maybe I'll see you again," I told him.

"I'd like that just fine." He gave me a little salute and left.

I stayed long enough to finish the bottle, then stood up and got set to leave. I wondered if Red had fallen asleep and almost nudged him when he suddenly stood up. It was the closest I'd ever come to touching him.

"Let's turn in, Red," I told him.

That mongrel dog proved himself useful again when we got outside of my room. I was about to open the door when he started growling and showing his teeth.

"What's the matter?" I asked him, but he kept staring at the door, growling, and then I knew what was wrong.

Somebody was inside.

I drew my gun and unlocked the door, swung it open just far enough for him to fit through.

"Go ahead," I told him.

He scampered through the door into the room, and I swung the door open and jumped in behind him.

He was barking at the person in the bed, who was holding the sheet up to her throat, staring at Red.

"Call him off!" she cried out. "Call him off!"

I relaxed and holstered my gun.

"What are you doing here?" I asked.

She took her eyes off of Red and looked at me.

"Waiting for you," she told me.

"What for?"

Angie realized by now that Red wasn't going to hurt her, so she dropped the sheet to her waist. Her breasts were larger than I had thought, but they were just as round and firm as I had figured. Her nipples were large and dark.

"What do you think?" she asked.

I approached the bed, and she said, "Not with him in the room," pointing to Red.

"Sorry, boy," I told him. I wasn't sure he'd leave if I told him, but he seemed to sense that neither of us wanted him there, so he turned and walked out the door.

I closed it behind him, then approached the bed again.

"Remember," I told her. "I'm a wounded man."

"Sit down," she said, holding out her arms, "and let me do the rest."

I sat on the bed and she began to unbutton my shirt. When she had helped me off with it, she kneeled behind me and began rubbing her breasts against my back. They were incredibly hot, and the tips felt like they were scraping.

"Ever since that night in the Linquists' house," she told me, whispering in my ear, "I've wanted you." I felt her hot mouth on my neck, across my shoulders. Gradually, she moved around me and pasted her mouth to mine. Her tongue was like a flame in my mouth, as her hands worked on my pants.

"The boots first," I told her.

She presented me with a view of her bare behind while she worked my boots loose. When she got the first one off I planted my bare foot on her right buttocks and

helped with the other one. When she had me totally naked, she pushed me down on my back and said, "Relax.
I'll do it all."

She took my long erection in her hands and began to
massage it.

She swiped at the swollen tip with her tongue a couple
of times, then took it in her mouth. I hadn't found many
women willing to do that, but the ones that had seemed
to be the young ones.

I went tense all over as she worked me in and out of
her mouth, and when I was about ready to explode she
let me slide free and straddled me. She felt slick and hot,
and she raised her hips and impaled herself. There was
a sharp intake of breath from both of us, and then she
began to ride me, slowly at first, but increasingly faster.

"Mother of God!" she cried out, then repeated the
same thing in Spanish. She did that a few times, saying
something in English, and then repeating it in Spanish.

Still riding me, she leaned over so I could take her
nipples into my mouth, first one, then the other. Then,
squeezing her breasts together, I took them both into my
mouth, sucking and biting them until I thought she
would go crazy. When her time came she sat straight up
on me and ground herself down on me, harder and
harder, biting her lips so she wouldn't scream. Then,
when I shot inside of her, she did scream, but with her
mouth closed, the cords on her neck standing out.

She collapsed on top of me, careful of my shoulder at
all times. Her tongue found its way into my mouth and
I bit it lightly, then sent mine into her mouth. She bit
mine hard and I reached around, cupped her bare buttocks, and pinched them both hard.

She squealed into my mouth, and rubbed her hands
over my chest.

"It was worth the wait," she told me.

"And it's better when I can take a more active part,"
I assured her.

"Oh, it was fine," she told me. She bent her head and began to lick my nipples. "Mmmm," she moaned, licking them, then moving down my body, licking my belly, and then lower still, moaning the whole time. In a few minutes I was hard as a rock again, and she moved up and impaled herself again.

This time, instead of starting out slow, she began fast and kept pumping and pumping, tireless in her quest for pleasure, until we were both ready to scream, and then collapsed on top of me again.

"I wondered if you could do it again so soon," she said.

"Only with the right provocation."

"Pardon?"

I put my good arm around her and said, "Only with the right person."

"You are sweet," she said, and kissed me, deeply and wetly.

Eventually she climbed off me and lay next to me.

"And what was all of that for?" I asked.

"I could say it was a thank you," she told me, laughing, "but that would be a lie. I came here because I wanted to make love to you, and I have wanted ever since that first night, when we were lying together among the bodies of those dead Indians." She realized what she had said and covered her mouth with both hands. "Oh, is that—how do you say, morbid?"

"That's how you say it, but I find it more flattering than morbid," I assured her.

"I am glad. I would not want you to think badly of me."

"I don't," I told her.

"That is good."

She reached between my legs and began to do things designed to bring me to life, but what she found was deader than—well, was pretty limp.

"No use, eh?" she asked, teasing.

"I haven't been well," I told her.

"Ah, tomorrow's another day," she said, and hopped out of bed. I watched as she began to dress. She bent over to pull on her pants and her bare breasts swayed, occasionally knocking together. It was a thoroughly enjoyable experience, watching a healthy young girl dress —almost as enjoyable as watching a healthy young girl undress.

As she tucked in her shirt she said, "Oh, I almost forgot. My father would like you to come to the Rancho for dinner tomorrow. You can make it?"

"I can't think of anything else I have to do," I told her, truthfully. Or, I added to myself, anything I'd rather do. "I'd like to meet your father."

"Yes," she said, "I'm sure you would."

She came over to me, bent down and kissed me long and hard.

"Mmmm," she said, her lips still against mine, "after that I shouldn't leave." She flicked her tongue across my lips, then stood up. "But I must. You will come to the Rancho at seven, yes?"

"I'll be there," I promised.

"Good."

She started for the door, then turned and said, "I cannot wait until you heal."

"That makes two of us."

She opened the door, started to walk out, then stopped short and backed up.

"Were you listening at the door, you naughty dog?" she demanded.

Red skulked in, looking embarrassed, if a dog can look embarrassed.

"You should teach him some manners," she scolded me, and left.

I looked down at Red and told him, "I don't know about you, pal, but I'm going to sleep good tonight."

I did, too.

19

Angie's visit had served to loosen up a lot of my tension. I slept real good, and when I woke my body felt totally relaxed. I almost hated to get up and ruin it, but my stomach began growling.

I swung my legs off the bed, and damned if they didn't still feel weak. I got up and poured some water from a pitcher into a basin and washed up, then got dressed. I was going to have to find ways to kill another day while I waited for evening to come, when I'd dress for dinner at Rancho Soto.

I wondered if anyone else would be there, or if it was to be a private dinner party.

How should I play it? I wondered, walking downstairs with Red at my heels. Should I come out and ask Soto what the story was, or wait until he brought it up?

Red and I had a long, leisurely breakfast. I again went through two pots of coffee. That was the one thing I missed while I was traveling, good coffee.

Afterward, I decided to kill two birds with one stone. I'd take Duke out and give him some exercise, and at the same time get a look at Rancho Soto.

I went over to the stable and saddled the big boy myself, just to see if I could do it with my bad shoulder. It was something of a struggle, but I got it done.

"C'mon, big boy," I told him, leading him outside
"Let's stretch our legs."

Outside I climbed into the saddle, then asked Tic
which way Rancho Soto was.

"You are going there, Señor?" he asked.

"I've been invited to dinner this evening," I told him
and he looked impressed. "I just want to make sure
will know how to get there."

He directed me south of town, pretty much in
straight run for about three or four miles. He said I'd b
on Rancho Soto land long before I came in sight of th
house.

"I'm impressed," I told him.

"Oh, you will be, Señor, I assure you," he said happi
ly.

I thanked him and the three of us headed south—me
Duke, and the mongrel Red.

My shoulder felt pretty good and, once we got out c
town, I set Duke off at a run. Nothing could touch th
big guy when he got going, but I didn't let him run fu
out, just enough to stretch his legs. I looked behind an
saw Red running freely behind us. I wondered how he'
be able to keep up if I did let Duke run full out. Mayb
we'd find out one day—that's if Red didn't find himsel
someone to follow before then. As quickly as he adopte
me, he could also abandon me.

"Okay, big boy, let's walk awhile," I told the bi
black, reining him in.

I didn't come to any fences; the Soto spread was ap
parently so vast they couldn't fence it all in. If what Tic
had told me was right, I was on Soto land right now.

And it was rich-looking land, too. The kind of land
once thought I would have. Oh, nothing this grand, ju
a small spread of good land, and Jenny as my wife.

That was thirteen years ago. Now it was just some
thing that might have been, could have been, mayb

even should have been. Was it even something I wanted anymore? I hadn't thought about it for so long, until recently.

I relaxed in the saddle and thought about what I wanted from Jenny after thirteen years.

I didn't know that I wanted anything from her. I just wanted to find out where she was, and what she had been doing, so I'd never have to wonder about it again.

I just wanted to know that she was all right, and happy.

I was awakened from my reverie by the approach of several riders. Instead of explaining what I was doing on Rancho Soto land I chose to hide behind a clump of trees, avoiding contact with the riders, who I assumed were ranch hands.

From my vantage point I made out six of them. Three of them were my poker buddies from the previous evening, including Joe Bags. I watched as they topped a rise, then disappeared behind it.

I wondered how far away the main house was, but I wasn't curious enough to keep riding. I assumed that if I did keep riding I'd come to it, so that would be the route I'd take that evening.

"Let's go back, Duke," I told the big boy, wheeling him around and heading back to town.

When I got back to town I wanted to satisfy my curiosity about the dinner invitation I'd gotten that evening, so when I turned Duke back over to Tico, the livery man, I went back to Dr. Montoya's office.

Luckily, he was in.

"What can I do for you, my friend?" he asked.

"Oh, I thought maybe you'd take a look at my shoulder. It's been kind of stiff."

"Well, that is to be expected, but come and I will have a look," he instructed.

He removed the dressing and looked at the wound.

"Very good," he told me. "No seepage of blood whatsoever. Excellent. I will put on a new dressing."

While he was doing that I said, "I had a talk with the sheriff yesterday. Seems he thought I was bothering some of the townspeople."

"I also spoke to him," he told me. "He was only doing his job, which he does very well, by the way."

"I'm sure he does. You know, I didn't even get his name while I was talking to him."

"It is Wakeman, Sheriff Bill Wakeman."

"How'd an American get to be sheriff of a Mexican town?"

Montoya only shrugged, saying, "He was the man for the job at the time. There, the new dressing is on."

"Thanks, Doc," I said, slipping my shirt back on. I watched his eyes when I said, "I guess I'll be seeing you tonight at Rancho Soto."

He frowned at me, studying me hard.

"You know, for dinner?" I prodded.

"Ah, yes, for dinner. Of course, I will see you there," he finally said, as if I'd reminded him of something that he'd forgotten about.

Outside I felt a certain amount of satisfaction in finding out what I wanted to know. I was going to Rancho Soto for dinner, so was the doctor, and very likely so were some other people. Apparently, Soto wanted other people around us when we met.

I assumed he wasn't intending to apologize.

I went to the cantina for a drink and found Joe Bags also indulging.

"Buy you one?" he asked as I entered.

"Just beer," I told him. "Wash away the dust."

"Been out riding?"

"Exercise, for both me and my horse."

"A big black, isn't he?" he asked.

"Yeah," I said, picking up my beer, "he is. How'd you know?"

He hesitated, then said, "I saw you out riding on Soto land a little while ago."

"Did you. I thought I hid myself pretty well."

"Oh, you did. I was the only one who saw you. Beautiful animal, that horse of yours. Fast?"

"The fastest I've ever seen or ridden."

He nodded.

"Soto's got a stallion he's pretty proud of. Plans on racing him. I'd like to see him hook your black."

"I'll keep it in mind."

He finished his drink and ordered another one. Leaning his elbow on the bar he asked, "You included in this dinner party I'm hearing about at the ranch?"

"I am, but I didn't know it was a party."

"Oh, yeah. The old man is so glad to have his daughter back that he's throwing a regular wing-ding."

"Hands invited?" I asked.

"Hell, no."

"Sorry to hear it. I would have liked to know I was going to see a familiar face tonight."

"You will," he told me, tossing off his next drink. "I gotta go, Clint. See you around."

"See you."

So I was going to a party, eh? Why hadn't Angie told me that last night. Did she want me to think that it was just a dinner to thank me? I'd ask her tonight when I saw her.

I sat at a table, drinking beer and toying with a deck of cards for the afternoon. I couldn't scare up a poker game, and eventually figured I'd better lay off the beer if I didn't want to fall off of Duke's back on the way to Rancho Soto. I decided to go back to the hotel, take another bath—two in one day was unusual for me—and get ready for the party.

Red followed me to the hotel and into the room where my bath was waiting. I wondered what I should do with him when I went to the party. Should I let him trail along? I decided to leave him in my hotel room, which I knew he wouldn't like, but I felt that would be the best way. I had never seen Red react to a large crowd of people, and I didn't want any surprises.

After dressing in my room, I told Red, "I've got to leave you behind this time, boy. I hope you don't mind too much."

He stared at me, cocking his head to one side, as if trying to understand what I was saying.

"Don't give me that," I scolded him. "You haven't had any trouble understanding me up to now."

I walked to the door and he started to follow.

"Stay there, Red. I mean it," I told him. He stopped in his tracks, and I opened the door, slipped out and closed it quickly behind me.

I could swear that while I was saddling Duke, the big black horse was looking for that mongrel dog.

"Not this time, big boy," I told him, swinging into the saddle. "It's just you and me tonight."

I took the same route I'd taken that afternoon, and when I reached that rise and the clump of trees, I kept on going. Before long I came in sight of the house, which surprised me by its size. It was all lit up and there were people arriving by buggy. I had not imagined anything that elaborate, that big.

There were hands out in front of the house, taking horses from people who arrived on horseback, and buggies from those who arrived that way.

I got off Duke and one of the men came over and took the reins from me.

"Take good care of him," I told him.

The man was Mexican, and he looked at Duke and patted his massive neck.

"It is an honor to handle such a horse, Señor," he told me.

"Make sure you're worthy of it, then," I warned him

"Si, Señor."

I ascended the front steps and went into the house, found myself in a large entry hall half filled with people. I took off my hat and held it in my hand, looking around for a familiar face, or something to drink.

"I'm glad you came," Angie said, handing me a glass of brandy, and then hooking her arm in mine.

"You didn't tell me it was going to be a party," I told her.

"I wanted it to be a surprise," she answered.

She was breathtakingly lovely. Her hair was loose around her shoulders, and her full lips were colored red. She wore a lime green gown of some kind of filmy material, cut daringly low in front.

"You look beautiful," I told her.

"I dressed for you."

"I'm glad I was on your mind," I told her. She squeezed my arm in reply.

"Let's see if we can't find my father in this crowd," she said, tugging at my arm. "He's anxious to meet you."

"I'm anxious to meet him," I told her, truthfully.

"We might also run across my stepmother."

"Stepmother? I didn't know—"

"Oh, I did not tell you?" she asked, and I had the impression she was feigning surprise. "My mother died nearly twelve years ago."

"How?"

"She was ill. She was a frail woman, and she succumbed to her illness. My father's new wife is much stronger."

"They married recently?"

She shook her head. "Over nine years ago—almost ten."

But still new to Angie. I sensed there was no love lost between stepmother and stepdaughter.

"Who are all these people?" I asked her.

"They are friends of my father's," she explained. "They come from all over Mexico, to remain in my father's good graces."

Apparently, Señor Soto was muy powerful, and everybody knew it. Then again, if no one knew it, he wouldn't have been all that powerful, would he?

"There's Doctor Montoya," she pointed out. We walked over to talk to him, arm in arm—which did not escape his notice.

"Mr. Adams, good evening."

"Good evening, Doctor. Enjoying yourself, I hope."

"Oh, yes indeed. I always enjoy myself at Señor Soto's parties," he informed me. "And how is your shoulder feeling?"

"Oh, it's fine, just fine, Doctor."

"That is good." Turning to Angie he said, "Señorita, you are looking very lovely this evening—and, if I may be so bold, very happy."

"Happy to be alive, Miguel," she told him, "and happy to be with the man responsible for my being alive."

"Of course, I cannot blame you for either. Excuse me, please, I must speak to someone."

We continued to circulate, and I met some other people.

"Who's the man in the uniform?" I asked, pointing across the floor to a silver-haired man wearing the uniform of the Mexican army.

"Captain Hernandez," she told me. "He is soon to be a general."

"From captain to general?" I asked. "That's quite a jump."

"I do not claim to understand politics," she told me. "Let us go out in the back and see if my father is there."

"Fine. Lead the way."

The back was also packed with people, and this crowd

was eating. I wondered if anyone had told the people inside that there was food being served. Perhaps the crowd was being fed in shifts.

"There he is," she cried out finally, pulling through the milling crowd.

At last, I was to meet the man who was very likely attempting to block me at every turn in my search for Jenny Sand.

He was very tall and erect, with gray hair, a gray mustache, and when I got closer I could see that he also had gray eyes. He was smiling broadly, and for a man over fifty he had very white teeth. He must once have been an impressively handsome man.

"Father," Angie called as we approached.

He looked up, saw her and waved. He said something to the people he was with, then started walking towards us.

"My child," he said, embracing Angie.

"Father, this is Clint Adams, the man who saved me from the Comanches."

Soto extended his hand and said, "Mr. Adams, I am Emmanuel Soto, and I am eternally grateful to you."

His grip was dry and firm and his eyes steady.

"I was happy to do it, sir," I told him.

"I hope you will let me repay you in some way."

"That won't be necessary, sir," I told him. I was annoyed with myself, because the man commanded respect, and I was responding.

"In a way, this party," he said, spreading his hands to indicate all of the activity around us, "is as much in your honor as it is in Angelique's."

"I'm just glad I was able to get her away safely," I said.

He patted my hand, which annoyed me even more, and said, "We'll talk about this later, Clint. Right now, enjoy the hospitality of my home, eh?"

"Thank you," I told him.

He found someone else who needed his attention and excused himself.

"I'm sorry," Angie said to me.

"For what?" I asked.

"He patronized you—is that the word?"

"If you mean what I think you mean, then he was condescending to me."

"I'm sorry?"

"That business about wanting to reward me, and calling me by my first name," I explained. "It's the kind of thing you do to someone you feel is not in your class."

"Class?"

"Someone you feel you are above, or better than."

"I am afraid that is my father's way with everyone he speaks to," she explained.

"Maybe I can set him straight, later."

"Please," she said, touching my arm. "Don't fight with him."

"I don't intend to," I told her, "but he likes to walk over people, and I'm not about to let him do that."

She took my empty glass from my hand and said, "I will get you another drink."

I watched her weave her way through the crowd and disappear into the house. To while away the time, I started appraising the women at the party. There were quite a few that were worth a second look, but for the most part the women were the wives of ranch owners in the area, and as such were older and less likely to attract the male eye.

That was when I saw her.

It was as if the crowd had suddenly parted, giving me a momentary glimpse of her standing there in the moonlight, and then closed up again, hiding her from me. The glimpse was brief, and it had been thirteen years, but I knew in an instant that it was her. Jenny.

20

My first impulse was to shout her name, but I quelled that urge and instead threaded my way to the spot where I had seen her standing. Naturally, when I got there, she had moved on.

I began to circulate, but she seemed to have disappeared. I was sure she hadn't seen me. I wondered whom she had come with.

"There you are," Angie's voice called out from behind me.

I turned and found her bearing down on me, drink in hand.

"I do not appreciate having to search for you while carrying your drink around," she told me, halfway serious.

"I'm sorry. I thought I saw someone I knew."

"A man?"

"A woman."

"Did you find her again?" she asked, handing me the drink.

"No, not yet."

That did not seem to upset her any.

"Then you will have to be satisfied with me," she reasoned.

Under any other circumstances, I thought to myself, I

would be more than satisfied with her.

"I saw my father again," she informed me. "He wants me to bring you to his study."

"Fine, lead on," I said, anxious for another conversation with Emmanuel Soto.

"I will take you, but you must promise not to fight with him," she told me.

"I won't lay a hand on him," I promised her.

"That is not what I meant," she scolded me, then turned and stalked off. I followed her into a part of the house was free of the crowd.

"The study is over here," she said, leading me to a pair of large oak doors.

"This is a beautiful house," I told her.

"My father built it," she said. She reached out and opened both of the doors leading to the study.

"Father, Mr. Adams is here."

"Bring him in," his voice said from inside.

She stepped aside. He was seated behind a large, ornate desk, and did not rise or offer me his hand again.

"You will allow us to speak privately, please," he told her. "Go and find your stepmother, and bring her here. I would like her to meet your rescuer."

"Yes, Father," she said obediently, and left, closing the door behind her.

"Mr. Adams," he addressed me, and I wondered if Angie had said something to him about calling me by my first name.

"Yes, Mr. Soto."

"Please, have a seat. I would like to discuss with you my desire to reward you for what you did for my daughter."

"I wish you would forget that, Señor," I told him.

"Ah, but I cannot. I appreciate too deeply what you have done for this house."

"As you wish. Oh, by the way, I bring greetings from

a friend of yours, in Texas."

"A friend, in Texas?" he asked, frowning. "Who could that be?"

"Jim Case," I said, watching his eyes. If the name was familiar to him, he hid it very well.

"Case," he repeated, frowning, "Jim Case. No, I don't believe I—"

"He's the sheriff in a small town called Red Sky," I told him. That rang a bell.

He leaned back in his chair and regarded me silently while he lit a cigar. When he had it lit he said to me, "Forgive me. Would you like a cigar?"

"No, Señor, what I would like are some answers."

"Yes, I imagine you would." He put the tip of the cigar in his mouth and rotated it slowly, drawing on it and allowing the smoke to escape from the sides of his mouth.

"Well?" I asked.

He seemed about to answer when there was a light knock on the door.

"Come in," he called out. I didn't turn around because I assumed it was Angie with her stepmother. I didn't like the idea of having to be polite for Señora Soto, just when I thought I might wring some answers from the Señor.

"Ah, my dear, come in. We've been waiting for you," Soto said, rising from his chair. I did the same, turning to meet the Señora.

"Mr. Adams, allow me to present my wife, Señora Jennifer Soto."

Yep, it was Jenny Sand.

21

"Mr. Adams, we were speaking of some reward for saving my daughter's life," he told me, while I stood there in stunned silence. "Well, this is the reward. You have been searching for Jennifer Sand for some time, now. The girl you knew as Jenny Sand ceased to exist over nine years ago, when she became my wife. I did not want you intruding on our lives, and that is why I attempted to thwart your efforts. Alas," he went on, raising his hand, "you rescued my Angelique from the Comanches, putting me in your debt."

He stood between Jenny and me. "Bueno, I am paying that debt now. This then is your reward. A few moments with my wife, Mr. Adams. After tonight, I owe you no debt. Please remember that."

He turned and walked out, without so much as a word to Jenny.

I stood there staring at her. She had matured into a woman of astonishing beauty. Her face had filled out, but her cheekbones were still high, her green eyes still shaped like a cat's, her hair red, just as I remembered. She was wearing a jade gown and a jeweled tiara.

"Hello, Jenny," I was finally able to say.

She seemed even more stunned than I was.

"Clint?" she whispered. She walked towards, taking small, hesitant steps. When she was with arms reach she put out one hand, touching my chest. I took her hand in mine and held it there.

"Clint, what did he mean, you've been searching for me?" she asked. "How? Why, after all these years?"

"It's a long story, Jenny . . . if we have time. Let's sit."

We sat down, close to each other, but not touching. She folded both hands in her lap while I told her about Harve Bennett, from the time I caught him, to the moment he was killed, so many years later.

"I realized you were another open chapter in my life, Jenny. I'd thought about you so many times over the past thirteen years—"

"—but you never looked for me," she finished.

I shook my head.

"My first thought was that you couldn't have loved me all that much if you hadn't waited," I explained.

"Oh, you were wrong, Clint. I loved you, more than I've ever loved anyone," she told me, then looked around quickly, realizing what she'd said.

"I know you went to Red Sky, Texas, Jenny. Mrs. Werth gave me your last letter."

"There were a few stops before Red Sky, but I settled there for a short while, until Emmanuel came to town one day."

"You came here with him?"

She shook her head.

"It wasn't like that. I did come to Blessed Gate with him, but not here, to the ranch. I taught school in town for a few months, while Emmanuel courted me. Then we got married."

"How old were you?"

"I was twenty-three when we got married, Clint. He was forty-nine."

"How could you—"

"He loved me, Clint. He was there, and promised he always would be. I never had to worry about whether or not he was going to get killed. He promised he'd always be there, and he has been."

"Well, good for him," I said, and she looked at me sharply.

"Don't—"she said.

"Do you love him?" I asked.

"That's a funny question for you to ask," she told me. "Do you think you have the right, after thirteen years?"

She was right about that.

"No, I don't suppose I do," I told her.

God, but she was beautiful! I wanted to take her in my arms. There was more to be said between us, but we were in the wrong place.

"Jenny, I wish—" I began, but I was interrupted when the doors opened and Emmanuel Soto walked back in.

"My dear, would you wait for me outside?" he asked her. He asked, but it wasn't really a request.

"Yes, Emmanuel," she said. One last look at me, and then she was walking out the door. Soto closed the doors behind her, then turned to face me. I stood up.

"Señor Adams, I am no longer in your debt. I would appreciate it if you would leave my house, and not attempt to see or speak to my wife again."

"Why? What are you afraid of?" I asked him.

"My wife is very precious to me, Señor. Do not force me to prove how precious."

"You're afraid of me, aren't you?" I asked him. "You're afraid of how she might feel about me, even after all these years. You've never been sure of your hold on her, have you?"

A muscle in his cheek twitched.

"I have asked you to leave my house, Señor. Please, do not force me to have you escorted."

"How would you explain that to Angelique?" I asked.

"I explain nothing to anyone!" he snapped. "Make your decision."

"Oh, I'll go, Soto, but if you're not sure of your wife now, you'll never be. Even if I'm gone."

I started for the door, then stopped next to him.

"I'm not sure who I feel more sorry for, Soto, you, or Jenny."

22

I had Duke brought around to the front of the house, and as I was mounting, Angie came running out the front door.

"Clint, where are you going?" she cried out, touching my leg.

"Ask your father, Angie. He told me to leave."

"You fought with him!" she accused. Stamping her foot she said, "I ask you not to fight with him."

"I didn't fight with him," I told her. "We just didn't see eye to eye on something."

"What?"

"You'll have to ask him."

"But—"

"I'll be in town, honey. If you want to talk to me, come and see me tomorrow."

"Clint—"

I wheeled Duke around and headed back to town. I wanted to sit in my room with a bottle and soothe my feelings. I had to speak to her again, away from Rancho Soto, if it could be arranged. My only access to the ranch was Angie; she'd hardly take kindly to acting as go-between between her stepmother and me. If I read my woman right, she had other plans for me, which was yet another problem.

Then I remembered another friendly connection to Rancho Soto.

Joe Bags. True, he was just a hand, and probably had never even spoken to Jenny, but he did have the run of the land, and could deliver a message to Jenny, if I decided to send one.

I'd have to talk to him tomorrow, as well as Angie.

Soto had ordered me from his house, but not from the town, which could prove an oversight on his part. Should he suddenly decide that he wanted me out of town—or even Mexico—I was sure he could bring a lot of pressure to bear, certainly from the sheriff, possibly even from the military.

I was going to have to talk to Jenny again. After a second conversation, I might just leave Mexico, willingly, saving myself a lot of grief.

Somehow, though, I doubted I'd be able to leave without encountering at least some grief. I was always a slow learner.

Red was right where I left him, just sitting in the middle of the floor. He stared at me accusingly when I came in, carrying nothing but a bottle of whisky I'd gotten from the saloon. I didn't know if he was mad because I'd left him locked in the room, or because I hadn't brought him back something to eat.

"I'm sorry, boy," I apologized to him, "but I've had a rough evening."

He didn't seem to appreciate that. He watched me while I drank half of the bottle, and then I couldn't take his staring any longer.

I dug a piece of beef jerky out of my saddle bag and threw that to him.

He was still chewing on it when I put the bottle down and fell asleep.

23

Red was in a foul mood when morning came, the piece of chewed-up jerky lying on the floor explained why. I scarcely remembered giving it to him. I took him downstairs and treated him to a double portion of eggs, which improved his mood greatly. My mood, however, was as dark as ever. I half expected the sheriff to interrupt my breakfast with orders to leave town. By now Soto must have realized he should have tossed me out of the country, and not just his house. I wondered if Angie had stood up to him and extracted from him some kind of story.

After breakfast I parked myself in one of the chairs out in front of the hotel, determined to wait there until either Angie or Joe Bags came to town, or until I received some kind of message from Jenny. She must have felt as I did, that we still had things to talk about. One way or another she'd get a message to me—if she didn't just up and come to town on her own.

And why not. As Señora Soto these past nine years, she could come and go as she pleased without explanation. That is, unless one night—last night—had served to take away nine years of privileges.

Round about noon at least one of my fears seemed about to come true.

I spotted Sheriff Wakeman coming down the street

towards me, and wondered if he was going to tell me that I wasn't exactly welcome in town anymore.

"Afternoon, Adams," he said, putting one foot up on the step, and his hand on his knee.

"Afternoon, Sheriff. Something I can do for you?"

"How was the party last night?" he asked.

"I'm afraid it didn't go all that well—for me, anyway," I told him.

"That's too bad."

"Yeah, I'm afraid me and Emmanuel didn't see eye to eye."

"That so? I would have thought he'd be plumb grateful for what you did," he said, looking as puzzled as he could without being downright comical.

"There was something else we didn't agree on, something personal."

"Oh, I see."

"Fact is, I kind of thought you might be coming over here to tell me to get out of town, or something. On Soto's orders, of course."

His face stiffened and he dropped his foot to the ground.

"I don't act on nobody's orders but my own, Adams. If I decided I wanted you out of town, I'd put you out myself."

"Yep, I imagine you would at that, Sheriff."

"As long as you keep your nose clean, I don't see any reason why you shouldn't stick around."

"Well, I'll sure keep that in mind, Sheriff. I surely will," I assured him.

He turned and headed back to his office without further word. For the moment it looked like I wasn't going to have to brace him. I wasn't looking forward to that because he was the law in town, and I made it a habit to respect the law, even if I didn't respect the man. In this case, though, I did respect the man.

I only hoped that his anger at my inference that he was Soto's man was real. Maybe I'd be able to count him on my side if the going got rough.

I sat out for another two hours and was starting to have my doubts when two of the people I was hoping would show up did so—together.

Joe Bags and Angie pulled up to the same spot and tied up their horses, but then they split up. Bags headed to the cantina, and Angie came towards me. She was halfway to the hotel when she saw me sitting out front.

I stayed where I was, waiting, and I didn't like the look on her face.

"I have to talk to you," she said, coldly.

"So, talk."

She duplicated Wakeman's position of two hours ago, one leg up and a hand on her knee.

"My father told me what you argued about."

"Did he?"

"He told me that you argued over the amount of the reward you each thought you should get. That's when I knew he was lying, because I know that you don't want any of my father's money."

"Do you know what I do want?" I asked.

"I think so."

"What?"

"I think you want his wife," she told me.

"You're wrong," I told her.

"And that's what my father thinks, too."

"Then he's wrong, also."

"Then what do you want?" she asked.

"I want to talk to her, Angie, that's all. We knew each other a long time ago. I want to talk to her, find out where she's been, what she's done, and if she's happy."

"I don't believe you," she snapped, her jealousy rising to the top, now. "I think you want her, and I can't understand why."

"Help me, Angie. Help me get to talk to her, away from your father's house. Bring her a message—" I started to say, grabbing for her hand.

She pulled her hand away as if mine were scalding hot.

"I will not carry your messages," she said between her teeth.

"Angie, don't be angry—"

"I will be as angry as I like," she told me. Her face was turning red and she obviously had a lot to say, but when it came out it came out in Spanish.

"Angie, I can't under—"

But she kept up the heavy torrent of Spanish, and from the tone I could just imagine what she was saying.

When she was finished she wouldn't listen to anything I had to say. She marched back to her horse, mounted up and rode out of town.

That left me with Joe Bags. I let all four legs of my chair hit the floor and headed toward the cantina.

Bags was sitting at a rear table, fiddling with a deck of cards. I grabbed a beer from the bartender and carried it to the table. He didn't look up until I sat down.

"Afternoon, Clint," he greeted.

"What brings you to town, Joe?"

"Nothing else to do, I guess. Rode in with the boss's daughter, Angelique."

"I believe I just saw her riding out," I told him.

"That so? Seems that girl can't make up her mind what she wants to do," he observed.

"I guess she's just like other women."

"Guess so."

We both chose that moment to drink some of our beer, and he lowered his glass first.

"How was the party?" he asked.

I lowered my glass. "That's what I want to talk to you about."

"You want to complain about the food? I can't help

you with that, Clint, you'd have to—"

"Do you know Mrs. Soto?" I asked, ignoring his attempt at humor.

"I've seen her, yeah."

"No, I mean do you know her? Have you met her, ever spoken to her?"

"Well, I—" he stopped to think a moment, aided by another swig of beer. "Yeah, I guess we've spoken once or twice. I think—yeah, I took her into town one time, carried packages for her." Shaking his head he added, "I told the foreman if he ever told me to do that again, I'd quit."

That brought up something I hadn't thought of before.

"Who's the foreman?"

"Guy named Melendez. He's been with the old man a long time, and has designs on the daughter."

"How about you?"

"What? The daughter? Sure, I'd like to take her out to the barn for a while, but that's it," he told me. "I ain't the marrying kind. I'm too young, and I'll be too young until the day I die."

"Okay, let's get back to Mrs. Soto."

"What's the sudden interest in the señora?" he asked.

So I told him.

He listened intently. "You still in love with her?" he asked when I was finished.

"No," I said, shaking my head. "That's what Angie—"

"Angie?"

"Angelique. That's what she thinks, too. I just want to talk to her, that's all."

"To Mrs. Soto."

"Right."

"Angelique won't help?"

"I'm not at all sure she likes her stepmother," I told him.

"Seems to me if she doesn't like her, helping you

would be a good way to get her in trouble with the old man."

"That's logical thinking," I told him. "You've got to remember she may be young, but she's still a woman."

He widened his eyes and said, "Believe me, I've noticed. So have all of the other hands."

"Anybody get close to her?"

He shook his head.

"A few have tried, but the old man doesn't like it. He seems to want her to marry Melendez."

"And how old is Melendez?"

"Oh, I guess he's almost fifty."

"Angelique can't be too happy about that."

"She don't confide in me." He finished his beer and waved for another round. "So what do you want me to do?"

"Are you afraid of old Emmanuel?" I asked.

"There ain't too many people in this world I am afraid of, Clint, and he ain't one of them."

"Okay. I'd like you to bring Jennifer a message for me. I want her to meet me—I'll write it down, this way you can slip it to her and the old man won't catch you talking to her."

I called to the bartender and asked him if he had some paper and a pencil. He searched around and came up with a slip of paper and a tiny pencil.

"This is going to look like some kid wrote it," I muttered, trying to hold the piece of lead.

I asked Jenny to meet me by the clump of trees I had hidden behind to avoid Joe Bags and the other riders. I signed the note simply with a letter "C."

"Here, take this," I told him, folding it and handing it to him. He looked at it, probably wondering if he should read it, then apparently decided against it and stuffed it into his pocket.

"Will you try and get that to her tonight?" I asked.

"I don't know what kind of an excuse I'll use to get near her," he told me, "but I'll try. I want something in return, though," he added.

"What?"

"I want to look at that special gun you carry," he told me, indicating my hip. "I've heard a lot about it."

"My gun," I said again. Not too many people have ever touched my gun. I had built it myself, from the basic Colt design, and the modifications I'd read about, from England. In this case, I didn't see the harm in letting him examine it.

"All right," I said, starting to pull it out.

"Not here. Let's go out back," he suggested, rising. I got up and followed him out the back exit.

"I come out here and shoot sometimes," he told me. There was plenty of room for it, and there was a corral and fence posts, where judging from the evidence—broken bottles, punctured cans—he often set up his targets.

He walked to the fence and found some whole and broken bottles, and also picked up some punctured cans, and set them all on the fence.

He came back, stood next to me and drew his gun. He fanned it, knocking all of the cans off the fence.

"Not bad," I told him, because it was probably what he wanted to hear. Shooting at inanimate objects never impressed me much.

"Can I try yours now?" he asked, holstering his.

I hesitated, then thought, Why not? I handed it to him butt first. He tested the weight and the balance, which were perfect for me.

"It looks like a Colt," he said, examining it closely.

"That's the basic design," I told him. "The modifications are the solid body and the double-action. Don't fan it, just squeeze the trigger."

"Don't cock it?" he asked, surprised.

"Just pull the trigger."

He pointed the gun and pulled the trigger, once twice. His first shot shattered a bottle, his second shot missed.

"Jesus, that's quick. It threw me off."

"Try it again."

He nodded, pointed the gun and pulled the trigger three times. He shattered a bottle each time.

"Nice," he commented, looking at the gun again. I reached out and took the gun from him before he could fire the last shot. I started to reload.

"You're careful," he told me.

"Not really. If I was I wouldn't have handed you my gun," I told him.

"You didn't let me fire the final round, though. And you were close to me the whole time I had it."

I finished loading it and put it back in my holster.

"There's a couple of bottles left," he pointed out.

"You take them. I don't shoot at bottles," I told him.

He smiled, drew his guns again, fanned it three times, taking care of the remaining three.

"That full speed?" I asked while he was reloading.

He looked at me and said, "I'll never tell."

I liked him, in spite of the fact that a gun seemed to be a toy to him, something to play with. That was the wrong attitude to take with something that could kill you.

"Will you deliver my message?" I asked him.

He holstered his gun and said, "Sure, I'll deliver it."

"Tonight," I reminded him. The note said to meet me early the next morning. I was sure that if Soto questioned her, she could tell him she was going for an early morning ride. People with that much money usually take early morning rides. In fact, that was how Angie got grabbed by the Comanches.

"Okay," he said, "It'll be tonight. Thanks for showing me the gun."

"Don't mention it."

24

Red tried to warn me, but they came out of the trees too fast, six of them, and all with guns in their hands. The one in front was bigger, older than the rest. I figured he was the foreman, Melendez.

"Step down, please," he said, motioning with his gun.

I could feel Duke's muscles bunch underneath me, waiting for a signal from me, but instead I did as he said. I climbed down and turned to face them.

Red was barking up a storm, but that didn't seem to bother them. Like Duke, I think the mongrel was waiting for some kind of signal from me.

I was gambling that they hadn't been sent to kill me.

Melendez said something in Spanish and one of the others relieved me of my gun. He threw it into the trees. Then Melendez spoke again and the same man punched me in the right kidney, dropping me to my knees.

"The Señor has sent us in reply to your message," Melendez told me.

I was still paralyzed by the punch in the kidney and could only watch as Melendez signaled to the other men and they all advanced on me. I felt only the first few blows. After that I got numb and kept fading in and out. I knew I was being struck, but couldn't feel anything so I didn't know where.

Then somebody hit me in my wounded shoulder and I screamed from the pain.

The last thing I remember was Melendez shouting, "Shoot the dog."

25

"Damn!" I snapped, because the first thing I felt when I woke up was the pain in my shoulder.

"Take it easy, my friend. You have opened your wound," Doctor Montoya told me, pushing me back down on my back. I hadn't even been aware that I'd sat up.

"I had some help," I told him.

Apparently I was in his office, lying on his table. I could feel some odd bumps and bruises, and I asked him about them.

"None of those are very serious," he assured me. "The worst thing they did was open your old wound."

As he tended to my shoulder I grew aware that we weren't alone in the room. I turned my head to the left, then to the right, and saw Joe Bags standing against the wall.

"Hey, Joe. Deliver my message?"

He stepped forward with his hat in his hand.

"To the wrong person, as you found out. I couldn't help it, Clint. Somebody saw us in town together. As soon as I got near the house, old man Soto was waiting for me. Took the message and held onto me until morning. I couldn't get to you in time to warn you."

"Your friend brought you in after he found you,"

Montoya told me, doing something to my shoulder that made it sting. "You are lucky that he did. You were bleeding badly."

"So bad I think you scared them," Joe said, taking up the story. "They must've thought they killed you, and they took off."

"Then I was right," I said.

"About what?"

"They weren't sent to kill me, just to warn me."

"I'd say they did that loud and clear," Joe told me.

"What about you?"

"Me?" he said, shrugging. "I was ready to quit that job anyway," he told me.

"You got fired?"

"I did."

"Ouch."

"Pardon," the good doctor said. He applied a dressing and told me that if I felt up to it I could stand up. He assisted me to my feet and I succeeded in staying there —none too steadily, but I was there.

Then I remembered the last thing I heard before going under.

"Red," I said.

"What?" Bags asked.

"The dog, and Duke, my horse."

They looked at each other, and the doctor turned away.

"Duke is fine. He ran off and wouldn't let any of them touch him," Bags told me.

"And the dog? I heard them say they were going to shoot him."

"They did," Montoya said, turning back, drying his hands. "I am not an animal doctor, but I did what I could, the rest is up to him."

"He's alive?"

He nodded.

"In the other room."

The other room was a large cupboard, and when I opened the door and let the light in, I saw Red lying on some blankets. He had a bandage wrapped around his side, and he could barely lift his head to see me.

Bags came up behind me.

"He must've chewed one of them up good. He had blood all over his mouth."

I nodded.

"He must've jumped them when they started pounding on me," I surmised.

"I can see where he'd be handy to have around. Why don't you pet him, let him know you appreciate it?"

"You want me to lose my hand?"

"What?"

"He doesn't like open displays of affection," I explained. "He knows I appreciate what he did—don't you, boy?"

He whined a bit and moved his head an inch.

"See?"

"I guess so."

"You get well, dog," I told Red. "You get well."

I backed out and closed the door.

"Bags."

"What?"

"My gun."

"I got it, Clint, don't worry."

I breathed a sign of relief.

"I guess I owe you for making you lose your job," I told him.

He shook his head.

"If I'd delivered the message like I was supposed to, I'd still have my job and you wouldn't have gotten new lumps. The way I figure it, we're even."

"Okay, we're even."

I walked over to where my shirt was and tried putting

it on. He gave me a hand when I got to the hard part.

"Thanks. What do you plan to do now?"

"Oh, I may just hang around and see how you make out. There are a lot of places I could go, but I'm in no rush to get to any of them."

"Got a stake?"

"I put away a few dollars. It'll hold me for a while."

"Good. I may have to borrow from you, so by all means stick around."

I buttoned my shirt and said again, "My gun?"

He pointed and I saw it hanging on a chair. I went over and got it and buckled it on. I felt better already.

"What's your next move?" he asked.

"Well, I still want to talk to Jenny, but I also want to have a talk with that foreman, Melendez. And now that I think of it, one of the hands along with him was one of those guys we played poker with."

"Which one?"

"I don't remember which is which. The one who called my full house with a pair of sixes."

"That was Jose Fuentes."

"Yeah, well, I owe him, too."

"You're building up quite a list of debts," he observed.

"And I'll pay them all off. That's a promise."

"I believe you."

"Now, if you'll walk real close to me so I don't fall down, I'll take you to the cantina and buy you a few drinks."

Bags smiled. "You're on."

26

Doctor Montoya recommended bed rest, and I vowed to do just that, after I got roaring drunk—as long as Bags was there to hold me up.

"You know what?" he asked, drunkenly.

"What?" I answered the same way.

"I think you're more mad that they shot your dog."

"He's not my dog," I said into my drink. "He just follows me around."

"I still think you're mad because they shot him."

"They're just lucky they didn't touch Duke," I said, and then I must have gotten a dumb look on my face, because he said, "Don't worry, I put Duke in the livery. He's being taken care of."

I was so relieved I had another drink.

"You drunk?" he asked.

"I've been drunker."

"Me too. Listen, Clint, if push comes to shove, I'll back your play."

Instead of pouring another drink I put the bottle down and looked at him.

"I hope it won't come to that, Joe. There's no reason for it."

"Well, just remember, I'll stand with you."

"Thanks."

"Another drink?"

"No, I've had enough," I said, turning my glass upside down. He thought about it a moment, then did the same with his.

"I hope you're not just looking for a rep builder," I told him. "I wouldn't take kindly to that."

"You think I just want to stand with The Gunsmith?" he asked. "Build a rep for myself? Imagine that," he said, staring at the ceiling, "I stood with the man who stood with Wild Bill. That's a rep builder, all right."

Having been put in my place, I decided to have another drink.

"Here's to those bastards who shot my dog," I told him, raising my glass.

He was about to drink to it and then stopped with the glass halfway to his lips.

"Hey, wait a minute. Ain't you the guy who keeps saying he *ain't* your dog?"

I downed my drink. "When they shoot him, he's my dog."

27

I didn't have Red to warn me this time, but I still knew there was someone in my room. I drew my gun, unlocked the door and kicked it wide.

"I'm sorry, Clint," Jenny said.

A woman waiting for me in my room again. This one was also on the bed, but completely dressed.

Jumping into the room hadn't done my shoulder any good, so I holstered my gun and used that hand to grab it.

"Did they hurt you?" she asked.

"They danced on my head, Jennifer, and on my chest and busted open an old shoulder wound—which I got saving the life of the daughter of the man who sent them to dance on my head . . . and chest . . . and—"

"Are you drunk?"

"I've been drunker," I answered, thinking that I'd played that scene not long ago.

She looked annoyed.

"I travel all this way to talk to you, sneak out of the house to do it, and you have to be drunk."

"Oh," I said, shutting the door behind me, "is Señora Soto displeased with me?"

"Oh, Clint—"

"Don't you think I have a right to be drunk?" I asked.

151

"It makes the pain easier to bear, you know?"

"Which pain is that?" she demanded.

I stared at her. "Don't tell me you think the same thing everyone else does."

"Which is?"

"That I want you."

She got one of those canny, female looks in her eyes and stood up. With her chest thrust out and her hands on her hips, she said, "You mean you don't?"

Before long we were on the bed and I was teasing the nipples of her large breasts with my tongue. The positions were the same as they had been with Angie, since I was still wounded, but for some reason the results were even more satisfactory.

"Oh, it's been so long," she moaned as she lowered herself on me, taking my shaft all the way to the hilt. "Oh, God, Clint, deeper! Deeper!"

When I came I felt as if I were being milked and when I was spent she was still riding my hard shaft up and down, tossing her head from side to side, getting satisfaction again and again, until she collapsed on my chest, her red hair tickling my nose.

"Did you come here for this, Jenny?" I asked her.

She took a moment, but eventually she answered with a muffled, "God, yes."

"Have you been happy these past nine years?" I asked.

"No," she answered, this time without hesitation. "I've been a prisoner."

"Why haven't you left?"

"To go where?" she asked. "I've never had anywhere to go, or anyone to go with . . ." she added, and let it trail off, the "until now" unspoken.

"Emmanuel has been kind—most of the time—and attentive, but for the past six years, he hasn't been able to . . ." she trailed off again and touched me to demonstrate what he hadn't been able to give her. "And even before that it wasn't very good."

"There are a lot of men on a ranch, Jenny."

"Believe me, I thought about it, more than once, but I've been faithful, Clint. I haven't been with another man since I married Emmanuel. Until today."

Her hand snaked down and encircled me, then began rubbing the length of me, up and down.

"You have no idea what it's been like," she said, rubbing me harder and harder. "I need this, Clint," she told me, "I need you."

She moved until I could feel the slick wetness of her dropping over me again, taking me inside, steaming inch by steaming inch. She began to move, her beautiful big breasts bobbing up and down as she rode me. I longed to turn her over and drive into her, but I settled for what I was getting. I watched her face as she bit her lip and tossed her head, a look of pure rapture on her face.

"Oh, oh, God!" she cried out, and once again she collapsed against me.

When she was dressing she suggested, "Just hang around town, Clint, don't come near the house. Don't give Emmanuel any excuse to send his men after you again." She came to the bed and kissed me hard. "Don't worry, darling, I'll get word to you and let you know when I can get away. Meanwhile, just rest up and get well." She kissed me again and whispered, "I love you. I always have."

She didn't wait for me to answer her, which was just as well. I didn't know what my answer would have been.

28

Hang around town, she said. Rest up and get well.

And then what? I asked myself the next morning. Was she going to keep me around to provide what the old man couldn't? I couldn't see spending the rest of my life waiting for a day when we could meet, with a week, maybe two or three in between, just for a roll in the hay.

Next time we were together there would have to be less sex and more talk, I vowed.

Sure, just get her to keep her clothes on.

Something was missing at breakfast that morning, and it took me a while to realize what it was.

That mongrel dog. Breakfast wasn't the same without him. Joe Bags—who'd taken a room in the hotel—made a poor replacement. Hell, he didn't even like eggs.

"Steak," he told me, "whenever I can get it. That's all I eat."

"Goes good with eggs," I suggested, but he just made a face and popped a large chunk of meat into his mouth.

"What's next?" he asked after breakfast.

"My second pot of coffee," I told him. "Whenever I can get it, I always have two pots."

"So, what now?" he asked, after the second pot was gone.

I wondered if I was going to have Bags following me

around too, now. When Red got back on his feet, one of them was going to have to go.

"Let's go over and see how Red is doing," I suggested.

"Who?"

"The dog."

"Oh, okay."

Montoya answered the door himself and led us to his new patient.

"He's responding well," he told me. "I think he'll be all right."

"That's good. Thanks, Doc."

Outside Montoya's office Bags asked me, "Now what?"

I stopped in my tracks, exasperated, and not wanting to show it.

"Bags, how about not asking me that anymore?" I asked.

"Okay, okay, don't get testy. Man, you must have had a rough night."

I looked at him sharply, to see if he knew more than he was letting on. Had he seen Jenny leave my room last night? I didn't think so. His remark seemed innocent.

"Look, let's go over to the cantina. You can sit and drink while I sit and think."

"I'm for that," he agreed. "It sounds like I'm getting the best of the deal."

He was right about that. While he sat and drank with his mind totally free, I sat with my back against the wall, staring at the same drink for hours, while my mind literally whirled.

Actually, I had accomplished what I had set out to do. I found Jenny, and I had found out what happened to her after she left Stratton, Oklahoma.

My other concern had been whether or not she was happy, and I had gotten my answer to that question, too. She wasn't happy.

Now, I had never given any thought to what I would do once I had gotten all my answers, and I never figured on what I would do if I found her and she was unhappy. Realistically speaking, however, was that really my problem? I mean, I had all my answers, so why didn't I just sit back and wait for my wound to heal, and then leave town and go on with my life?

Good question.

I must have made some kind of a derisive noise with my mouth because it caught Bags's attention and he asked, "What's the matter?"

"I'm just wondering what's holding me here," I told him.

"Well, your shoulder, for one thing," he pointed out.

I touched it and replied, "Yeah, well, in a couple of days that won't be an excuse anymore, will it? Then what'll be holding me back?"

He shrugged, answering, "Nothing."

"Right."

"And if you don't mind, when you ride out I'll go along with you aways."

"Sure, why the hell not?"

Actually, I could have ridden out right there and then, but my shoulder had taken a beating, and would probably act up during the long ride back through Texas.

"Together we'd stand a better chance against Apaches and Comanches, anyway," I added.

"That's what I figure," Bags said.

"So that settles it, then," I said.

"It does?"

"Sure, three days at the most, and we'll pack up and ride out of this town."

"What about your debts?"

"I'll just have to make sure they're all paid off by then," I told him.

"How do you propose to get near the house?" he asked.

"I don't have to," I told him. "They have to come into town sometime, right?"

"Unless they have orders to stay out of your way."

"True, but then I have you."

"Me?"

"You know their schedule, their work habits. Couldn't you figure out where they would be at any given time of day?" I asked.

He thought a moment and then said, "I suppose so. Let's see, right about now Jose would be working on that south fence, mending it. Melendez is probably checking on the stock—"

"See? We could probably find them any time we want."

"I guess, but why do you think they were given orders not to kill you?"

"I think this sheriff is on the up and up," I explained. "I don't think he's in Soto's pocket—or at least not all the way in. To kill me would bring them some trouble from him, and I think Soto would like to avoid that."

"Then why not report the incident to the sheriff?"

"You've got to look at it from his point of view, Bags. I was on private property, even though I could claim ignorance of that fact, but Soto could still file a complaint against me for that. Or the six men who jumped me could claim that I started the fight."

He snorted.

"That'd be ridiculous!"

"Wakeman would still have to entertain their complaint," I explained.

Shaking his head he said, "Boy, I'm glad I'm not a lawman."

"The job has its points," I told him. "Just like any other."

"Well, you'd know better than me," he conceded.

A thought struck me then, and I made a quick decision. I stood up and he asked, "Now where you going?"

"Just stay here," I told him. "I've decided to talk to the sheriff, anyway."

"After what you just said?"

"I'm not going to file a formal complaint, I'm just going to talk to him, as one lawman to another."

"Ex-lawman," he reminded me.

Only someone who had never worn a badge could make a statement like that.

29

"And you don't want me to take any kind of action?" Wakeman asked, after I'd told him the story.

"What action can you take?" I asked. "It's my word against theirs, and they could even get twenty witnesses each to swear that they were on the ranch when I claim they were beating me up."

"I see what you mean," he said, scratching his head. "So why are you telling me all this?"

"Because I think you're for real, Wakeman," I decided to tell him. "I think that if Soto broke the law and you knew it, you'd arrest him—if you had proof."

"Well, you're right about that. Thanks for the vote of confidence," he said, wryly.

"A couple of bad experiences can shake your confidence," I told him, referring to my experiences in Stratton and Red Sky. "You've renewed my faith in the law, Wakeman."

"Well, gee—" he said, feigning embarrassment.

"Anyway, I just wanted you to be aware of what happened," I said, heading for the door.

"Adams?"

"Yeah?"

"You're not planning to do anything stupid—"

"Of course not," I told him, opening the door, "didn't

161

I just finish telling you what respect I had for the law?"

"Just remember what you said about me. I don't want any Rancho Soto hands turning up dead. That's a warning."

"I hear you, Sheriff," I told him, an answer which really didn't mean anything, and he knew it.

He shook his head and said, "Just do me a favor, Adams?"

"What?"

"Don't litter the streets of my town with the objects of your revenge."

"Sure."

"I'd hate to have to go up against The Gunsmith," he told me, "but this badge says I will if I have to."

"I believe you, Sheriff."

And I did, too, but I was going to pay my debts, anyway, and hope that it never came to a facedown with Wakeman.

I went back to the cantina, where Joe Bags had a fresh beer waiting.

"Thanks," I said, sitting down to a sip.

"So, what happened?"

"We both made hardcase noises at each other," I told him.

"What'd he say about your friends?"

"Nothing. We both agreed there wasn't much he could do. I told him I just wanted him to know what was going on."

"Whose side will he take if push comes to shove?" he asked.

"The law."

"Shit," he said, picking up his beer mug, "I thought he'd be with us."

30

My biggest problem over the next few weeks was keeping a tight rein on Joe Bags. He wasn't happy just waiting around. He wanted either to take some kind of action against the Rancho Soto boys, or just up and leave town. Everytime I told him to go ahead and leave, he'd quiet down and tell me that he'd wait a couple of more days.

My other problem was Jenny. She'd managed to visit my hotel room four times during the ensuing weeks, and each time she was wild, not giving me a chance to talk. The last time she'd visited me had been the worst, conversation wise, because my wound was healed enough for us to change positions, and I was so caught up in our passion that we had barely spoken at all.

After she left that night, I spent my time wondering what was happening to me. I seemed to be caught between my past and my future, not sure which way I wanted to go. And I was going to have to make a decision.

Only a fool goes back when he can go forward. I knew what was behind me, and a lot of it I didn't like. What lay ahead was mystery, and mysteries were meant to be solved.

Forward it would be, then, and the next morning I'd

start on my way by paying the first of my debts.

The next morning at breakfast, when Joe Bags started complaining about the lack of activity, I surprised him with a new answer.

"You're right."

"I can't be sitting around here much longer, Clint. I've got to—" he stopped short and stared at me, realizing that my answer had not been the same one he'd been hearing for weeks. "What did you say?"

"I said, you're right, Bags. It's time we started making some moves."

"Do you feel up to it?" he asked.

"The shoulder's fine."

"I didn't mean your shoulder," he told me.

I frowned at him.

"What did you mean?" I asked.

"How's your head?"

"Nothing's wrong with my head, Bags," I told him. "What are you getting at?"

"Nothing. I've just noticed that these past few weeks your head hasn't been particularly straight."

He was more observant then he let on, and I knew he had to be talking about Jenny and me. His question was a good one. Was my head straight now? If he was going to stand with me, he deserved an answer, and an honest answer, at that.

"You're right, Bags. My head hasn't been on straight the past few weeks, but it's okay now."

"Is it?"

"Yes, it is."

"I'll take your word for it, Clint. And I'm glad to hear it."

So was I.

Jenny was a part of my past, and it was time I stopped letting her interfere with my future.

"Are we going to pay a visit to Melendez and the others?" Bags asked eagerly.

"I think it's about time," I answered.

"When?"

I poured myself a cup of coffee and said, "After my second pot."

31

Bags led us to the southernmost part of Rancho Soto, where he said Jose Fuentes would be working.

"How can you be sure?" I asked.

"It's a stretch of fence that is the least important of all the miles of fence surrounding Soto land. Repairing it is always left to one man—or at least, it has been for as long as I've been here. Jose doesn't like people, Clint. Any job that can be done alone, he volunteers for. He'll be there, if he's anywhere."

So I followed Bags and his roan, with Red bringing up the rear. Red had dropped a lot of weight during the period of his healing, and this was his first real outing since his injury, but he was keeping up very well. His enthusiasm at being out again, and able to run, overcame the weakness he felt as a result of his wound. I was glad to see the bad-tempered mongrel back on his feet.

Bags reined in his roan and I pulled Duke up beside him.

"Over that ridge," he said, pointing ahead of us, "is where the damaged stretch of fence is."

"I hope it hasn't already been repaired," I said.

He was tactful enough not to point out that, if it had been, the missed opportunity would be my fault.

"I'll ride straight over the ridge," he suggested, "and you come over from the left. I'll keep his attention distracted so you can come up behind him."

"Won't he know why you got fired?" I asked.

"No, I don't think so. I'll tell him I'm on my way to —to anywhere, but away from here. See you soon."

"Good luck."

"Oh, you better keep the dog out of sight."

"You tell him."

He looked at Red and started to say, "Keep out of—" then he stopped and looked at the sky. "Now he's got me talking to a dog." He spurred his roan and I watched as he started up the ridge.

"C'mon, big boy," I told Duke. We started up the ridge at an angle, the distance between Bags and myself growing larger the higher up we got. Red seemed to sense the urgency for silence, and remained behind Duke, dutifully following in his hoofprints.

As I was about to top the ridge I stopped. I wanted to give Bags time to ride down to Fuentes and engage him in conversation—and get his back turned towards me.

"Okay, Duke, let's go up, slow," I told the big guy, and he started towards the top. When we got there I was able to look down at Bags, still on his roan, talking to a man whose back was to me. Bags was waving his hands around, probably complaining about the lousy treatment he'd gotten from Rancho Soto. As we started down the other side, I could see Fuentes nodding his head, apparently agreeing with him. For a big horse— the biggest I'd ever come across—Duke could walk like an Indian pony.

Eventually, we came within earshot and Duke came to a halt.

"No, actually I'm not traveling alone, Jose. I brought a friend with me."

"Si?"

"Yeah, maybe you know him," Bags told him, then looked past Jose directly at me. Following the direction of his gaze, Jose turned and, smiling, looked at me. His smile turned to a slight frown as he struggled to remember where he'd seen me before. I got down from Duke's back and walked over to the Mexican ranch hand.

"Hello, Jose," I said.

"Do I know you, Señor?" he asked, still puzzling. When I got into position I gave him a hint that would help him remember.

I swung a vicious right into his kidney, dropping him to his knees, causing him to gag.

"Remember me now, amigo?" I asked.

He was making all kinds of sounds, but none of them were recognizable as words, so I gave him a nudge with my foot.

"Si, si," he croaked.

"Good, now lie back and catch your breath, Jose," I told him, planting my foot on his chest and pushing him down. "That's more than you let me do."

He stayed on his back, making tortured sounds as he tried to breath. I knew how he felt, but I felt no sympathy for him.

Bags just sat on his horse, watching out for other riders, while I "talked" with Jose.

I squatted down next to Jose, who seemed to have no thoughts at all about going for his gun. The only thought on his mind right now was to get some air into his burning lungs.

"Go ahead, Jose, breathe, breathe deep. I'm going to ask you some questions, amigo, and every time I don't like your answer, I'm going to roll you over and give you another shot in the kidney. Comprende?"

"Aye, si, yo comprendo," he told me, grimacing with pain.

"Good. Now tell me what your orders were the day you and your amigos worked me over."

"Melendez—"

"And in English," I reminded him.

"I must go slowly in English," he told me, fearing another kidney punch should his answers be too slow.

"That's okay, amigo. I got time."

"Melendez, he say Señor Soto wants us to, uh, scare you away, maybe hurt you, uh . . . a leetle bit—"

"Did he tell you not to kill me?"

"Si, he says no kill."

"What was Melendez doing while you and your amigos were beating on me?"

"He stand a watch, he laugh—"

Somehow, that bothered me even more than if the foreman had also been throwing punches and kicks.

"Did you get paid extra for the job?" I asked.

"Si, cinq—uh, fifty dollars for each of us."

And Melendez must have gotten at least double that, I figured. Soto went for four hundred dollars or so just to scare me, not out of town, but into staying away from Jenny. I wondered how much he'd go for if he knew she'd been to my room those times.

"Okay, amigo, now I want the names of the other four men."

"Madre Dios—" he began, but I put a hand on him to roll him over, and he started rattling off names so fast I couldn't follow him.

"You catch those names?" I asked Bags.

"I got them, and I know them," he assured me.

"Good. All right, Jose, up we go," I told him, taking his arm and helping him to his feet. His horse was tied off a few yards away, and I pointed to it and told him, "Get on that horse, amigo, and ride."

He stood hunched over, holding the tender spot on his back with one hand.

"But, to where?"

"I don't care, Jose. Anywhere, just so long as I don't see you around Blessed Gate, or the Soto ranch anymore. Comprende?"

"Señor, my job—"

I put my hand on his shoulder and he flinched, misinterpreting my move.

"You'll get another job, amigo—somewhere else," I told him.

"Somewhere healthy," Bags added.

Fuentes looked from me to Bags a couple of times, then began to walk gingerly to his horse, muttering to himself in Spanish. We watched as he tried to mount his horse, finally making it on the third attempt.

"You let him off easy," Bags said, as I mounted Duke.

"I'm saving it for the end," I told him.

"Melendez?"

I nodded.

"And Soto."

"Man's just trying to keep his wife."

"Well, I don't like the way he goes about it," I told him. "Come on."

"Where to?"

"Back to town. We're going to make a list."

32

Five days later Bags and I were sitting in the cantina having a few beers late in the day when Sheriff Wakeman walked in. He looked around the room and when his eyes fell upon us it was evident that we were the ones he was looking for.

"Here he comes," I told Bags. Since my back was to the wall, his was to the front door, so he hadn't seen the sheriff walk in.

"Do you want to lie to him, or should I?" he asked.

"Just keep your mouth closed," I advised.

As Wakeman approached the table Red picked up his head and peeked out from beneath my chair. When he saw the sheriff he started to growl. He'd been growling at everyone but me since he got shot.

Wakeman had been coming around to that side of the table, but when he saw Red he changed his course and came around the opposite side.

"Hello, Sheriff," I greeted. "Pull up a chair and have a drink."

"I'll take the chair and pass on the drink."

"What's on your mind?"

"Have you heard about the accidents the boys from the Rancho Soto have been having lately?" he asked, looking at both of us.

Bags shrugged and I said, "Accidents, what kind of accidents?"

"Every kind. They've got one man with his arm busted up so bad they'll probably make a cook out of him, another with a leg broke so bad he's gonna limp for the rest of his life—he got dragged by his horse and doesn't remember how it happened. Another guy got his hand so mangled he'll never be able to hold a gun again."

I stared at him and said, "So, what's that got to do with us?"

"Nothing," he told me, "at least, nothing I can prove. If I tell you these guys' names, could you tell me if they were the ones who worked you over?" he asked.

"Sheriff, I don't know the names of the men who worked me over," I reminded him.

"Oh, yeah, that's right," he said. "I forgot."

"Yeah, you forgot." I leaned forward and asked, "What makes you think we've had anything to do with these accidents?"

"There haven't only been accidents," he told me. "One man has completely disappeared."

"Which one?" Bags asked.

"Jose Fuentes."

"I know him," Bags said.

"Yeah, well, nobody has seen him for five days, and no body's been found. He's just gone."

"Maybe he felt like leaving," I suggested.

"And these other fellers felt like having accidents?"

"Sheriff, I don't know anything about any accidents, and neither does my friend, here."

He looked at Bags again and said, "You used to work out on the ranch, didn't you?"

"That's right."

"What happened?"

"I got fired."

"Why?"

Bags looked at me and answered, "They didn't like the kind of friends I keep."

Wakeman looked at me and I shrugged.

"Adams, I'm asking you to remember what we talked about at the beginning of the week, and I'm hoping that there won't be anymore accidents involving the Rancho Soto boys."

"Just don't hold me responsible for any accidents, Sheriff," I told him, "if you can't prove anything."

We stared at each other hard for a few moments, and then he pushed his chair back and stood up.

"You'd do well to pick your friends more carefully, young feller," he told Bags.

"I'll do that, Sheriff. Thanks for the advice."

Wakeman gave us each one last hard look, then turned and walked out of the cantina.

"Sounds like the Rancho Soto boys are getting accident-prone," Bags said. Accidents that had been arranged by Bags and myself. I had told Bags that I wanted to make damn sure we didn't kill anyone.

"How about letting them know that it's you that's doing it?" he asked. "How else they gonna know why its happening?"

I had shaken my head at that one.

"Mexicans are suspicious people, Bags. They'll figure out why the accidents are happening only to the men who worked me over."

When the Sheriff was gone, Bags took out our list and crossed off the name of the man who had been dragged by his horse yesterday.

"That makes four," he told me, "and leaves Rogerio Gomez. After him it'll be Melendez."

Then Soto himself, the man who ordered me beaten. It had all started with my wanting to see Jenny and talk to her, but my revenge now had nothing to do with Jenny. I was simply working my way up the list to Soto, because I was not about to take a beating and let it go at that. It didn't even have anything to do with my reputation—which is what Bags thought—but simply my pride.

"We'll take care of Gomez tomorrow," I told Bags. "Why don't you go find something to do?"

"I think I'll go see one of Rosa's girls," he said, finishing his beer and standing up. Bags made a visit to Rosa's bordello three or four times a week. Sometimes being with him made me feel older than thirty-nine.

"Okay, I'll see you in the morning."

He nodded, and dug into his pocket for money for his drinks.

"I got it," I told him. He smiled, waved, and left.

I had sent him on his way because that morning I had received another note from Jenny, saying as they usually did: Tonight.

Tonight, I'd decided, was going to be the night that we would talk, really talk about why I had come to town and why, very soon, I would be leaving.

I dropped some money on the table and headed back to the hotel, with Red on my heels.

I wondered, as I had in the past, how Jenny was getting away from the ranch for these late-night visits, and how she was getting in and out of the hotel without being seen.

As we reached the hotel I turned and stopped, and Red stopped and stared at me. He was looking good since he'd begun getting exercise. He was still a little on the thin side, but looking much better and healthier.

"Tonight's one of the nights you spend in the stable with Duke, Red," I told him. He stood staring at me, head cocked to one side. "Don't pull that with me," I told him. "You understand every word I'm saying. Now go on, git!"

He seemed to heave a big sigh and then turned and headed for the stable. I was very pleased that the two animals had taken to each other so well. If Red was so intent on following me around for who knew how long, it was just as well they liked each other.

Even before I opened my door I knew she was inside. Her scent still hung in the hallway—and then as I opened the door, I realized that, although the scent was familiar, it wasn't Jenny's.

It was Angie's.

She was sitting up in my bed when I walked in, with the sheet held up to her chin.

"Hello," she said. I guess I must have looked surprised, because she said, "Why so surprised? Didn't you get my note?"

Her note? I had thought the note was from Jenny—or was Angie talking about another note, one that perhaps was still in my box downstairs?

"Where'd you leave it?"

"Downstairs, with the desk clerk. He said he'd put it in your box."

"I haven't been back here since morning, and I just walked past him downstairs. How've you been, Angie?"

She made a face and said, "Miserable, since we argued."

"Did we argue?"

Now she smiled sheepishly and said, "Well, I did. I'm sorry I got angry with you, Clint."

"That's all right, Angie, don't worry about it."

"Come over here so I can make it up to you," she invited, patting the bed with one hand.

"I don't think so," I told her.

"Why not?"

"It's not a good idea."

"Why not?" she insisted again.

"Well, aside from the difference in our ages, your

father wouldn't be too happy about this—"

"As far as the age difference, who cares?" she snapped. "There are more years between my father and Jennifer then there are between you and me. As far as my father not liking it, that doesn't seem to keep you from sleeping with his wife, so why should it bother you with his daughter?" she demanded.

I didn't know quite what to say to that, so she went on.

"Don't think I don't know where Jennifer has been going when she sneaks out of the house late at night. And I'll tell you something else. My father is no fool, he probably knows to. I don't know why he's letting it go on, but when he decides to put a stop to it you're going to be sorry."

As she was talking she got up from the bed and started dressing, bare breasts bouncing around as she angrily pulled her skirt on.

When she was dressed she stormed past me, then turned and snapped. "I hope he has somebody cut your cojones off!" She stormed out the door.

I was sorry I had hurt her and made her angry. Lord knows, I would have loved to go to bed with her, but I was trying to cut any and all ties I had to anyone in this town, including Jenny—which was something we'd talk about tonight. When it came time for me to leave, I didn't want anything holding me back.

There was a knock on the door and so little time had passed since Angie had left that I thought it might be her.

"Come in," I called out.

Jenny stuck her head in the door and looked at me.

"Oh, good," she said, "I'm not interrupting any-thing," and I knew that she had seen Angie leaving.

"Jenny—" I started, but she kept right on going with-out giving me a chance to speak.

"When I saw my stepdaughter leaving I figured if you were keeping both of us busy, why not somebody else, too?"

She shut the door behind her and put her back against it.

"I'm sure if you saw her leave you must have seen that she wasn't exactly happy."

"Couldn't you perform to her satisfaction?"

"If all you want to do is insult me, Jenny," I told her, "you can turn around and walk right out."

"I'm sorry, darling, I was jealous. What did she want?"

"She wanted to tell me that she knew about us, and that she thought her father did, too. What do you think?"

She shrugged. "He may know. He's not a fool."

"That's what she said."

"Well, we both know the man pretty well, then."

She began to unbutton her dress and I put my hands on her shoulders and said, "No, Jenny."

She looked at me, puzzled.

"You don't want me?" she asked.

This had to be the first time in my life I ever turned down two beautiful women in five minutes.

"It's not that," I told her.

"Then what is it?" she asked, frowning. "Is it Angel— is it because she knows?"

"No, Jenny," I told her "it's because I know. I know, Jenny."

"You know?" she asked. "You know what, Clint?"

"I know that I shouldn't have come here looking for Jenny Sand, because what I found was Jennifer Soto. I loved Jenny Sand, and . . ."

"And what?" she demanded, sensing where the conversation was going.

"And I don't love Jennifer Soto," I told her. "They

are two different women, thirteen years removed from each other.''

"And I suppose you're the same?" she asked.

"No, Jenny, I'm not the same.''

"I'll say you're not,'' she said, turning her back and crossing her arms over her chest.

"What did you think the first time I came up here, Clint? Did you think I came up because I loved you?''

"Jenny, let's not—''

"No, let's, I insist,'' she said, turning back to face me. "Let's be honest with one another. That's all I wanted from you, Clint,'' she told me, pointing to the bed. "I'd been a good, dutiful wife to Manuel, even though he couldn't give me what I needed. When you came to town, when I saw you, I decided that I'd gone without for too long. That's why I came up here, and that's why I came up all the other times.'' She dropped her hands from in front of her chest and pulled her shirt open, popping a couple of buttons. Her breasts thrust themselves out at me, brown nipples hardened with desire—either that, or anger.

"Damn you, Clint,'' she snapped, "that's why I came up here tonight!''

She pulled the garment off and threw it to the floor. I watched as she angrily removed the remainder of her clothes, and then stood before me, glowing and naked.

She came to me, her flesh soft where it should be, and firm where it should be, and burning hot all over. She came to me, and I took her, because what else could I do?

33

"I'll be leaving soon, Jenny," I told her later.

She thought a moment, then said, "Take me with you, Clint."

"Jenny—"

She put her finger against my lips and said, "I'm not asking you to love me, Clint. I've wanted to leave for a long time, but I've never had the courage. If you would take me with you, I could gather up the courage to do it."

"Why don't you just tell your husband—"

"Tell him I want to leave him?" she finished. She stared at me, and then seemed to stare somewhere inside herself.

"Clint, I almost believe he'd rather kill me than let me leave him."

"If that were true," I told her, "then wouldn't he have had me killed instead of just having me beaten up?"

"Maybe I'm just being silly, I don't know. I am afraid of him. I would rather leave with you, and then contact him later."

I thought about it. There was no pretense of love, now, no tie to the past. She was afraid of her husband and was asking me to let her leave with me—not *take* her away with me, but simply to *let* her leave with me.

What was the alternative? If she gathered up the courage to leave alone, how could she travel through Indian country by herself?

She couldn't, not and get through alive.

"All right, Jenny, you can leave with me," I told her.

She rubbed her cheek against my chest and said, "Thank you, Clint. When?"

"When all my debts are paid," I told her.

"What?" she asked, not understanding.

"I'll let you know when."

34

"Your head is on crooked again," Bags told me at breakfast.

"You don't have to come," I said, ignoring his statement. "You can either leave before us, or after us."

Shaking his head he said, "Mark me crazy, but I'll leave with you. If her husband gets wind of it, you'll need help. He's got a lot of hands on that ranch."

I grinned at him and said, "Thanks, Bags."

"What about Gomez?"

"We'll do him today, just as we planned."

And we did. By afternoon, Gomez was in Doc Montoya's office with a broken ankle. He had been gathering strays from the mountains behind Soto land, and something had spooked his horse. Some of the cattle had been spooked also, and one of them had stepped on Gomez's ankle, breaking it. Bags and I just happened along and found him and brought him back to town.

At least, that's the story we told Wakeman.

"What were you doing out there?" he asked us.

"Just riding," I told him. "I guess whatever the reason, that man is lucky we were there."

"I wonder," Wakeman said, inspecting both our faces, "I wonder just how lucky he was."

"He was very lucky," Montoya said, coming out of his treatment room. "With that injury and no horse, he would never have made it back to town alive."

Wakeman nodded, then looked at us and nodded in a different way.

"You're lucky that man's not dead, Adams," he said.

"I'm glad he's not, Sheriff."

"You know, Adams, I always thought that you couldn't mix gunfighting and the law. You can't be a gunfighter and a lawman and be a good lawman. You're proving that to me right now. Men like you and Hickok should never have a badge pinned on their chest."

He turned around and went in to talk to Gomez. He was hoping that Gomez could implicate me somehow, but the Mexican wouldn't be able to. He hadn't seen me anywhere near his horse when it spooked.

"The sheriff seems to feel that you have something to do with this man's injury," the doctor remarked.

"He can't prove it, though," I pointed out.

"I see," he replied. "And did you?"

I started for the door, and Bags followed.

"Doc, if I admitted it to you," I told him, "then he would have proof, wouldn't he?"

"Es verdad," he admitted.

"It sure is," Bags said, and we went outside.

"I guess that leaves Melendez," he said outside. "It won't be as easy to predict his movements as it was the hands."

"I guess not," I said, only half-listening. I was thinking if it wasn't time now to get out, and forget about Melendez and Soto. I was also thinking about Wakeman's statement, about being a gunfighter and a lawman. I had never thought of myself as a gunman, but I had to admit that I did have that reputation, the same as Wild Bill did. How would history look at men like Bill, as a gunfighter, or a lawman? How would history look at me? How would I prefer to be remembered?

Since I was still alive, and not yet a part of history, that decision was still in my hands.

35

"What do you mean, we're leaving? We can't leave now?" Bags argued.

"Why not?"

"We're not finished with Melendez, and Soto."

"I've had enough of that stuff, Bags," I told him. "I just want to get out of this town, and out of Mexico."

"You want them to be able to say they ran you out?"

"I don't really care what they say," I confessed.

We were sitting at a table in the cantina with a bottle of rotgut on the table between us, and I grabbed it and poured myself a shot.

"Clint, what about your rep?" he asked.

"Why do you think a rep is so important?" I asked him.

"Maybe it's because I ain't got one," he answered.

"You want mine, Bags? Believe me, right now you're welcome to it."

He stared at me a few seconds. "I guess not," he admitted, pouring himself a drink from the bottle. "Seems to me you worked pretty hard for it yourself. I'll get my own, sooner or later."

"Maybe, Bags," I told him. "But don't count on me to help you to it. If that's why you're hanging on with me, I told you before, I won't take kindly to it."

He knocked off his drink and said, "Well, seems to me lightin' out with you ain't likely to build me any kind of rep, but I'm still doing it, ain't I?"

"Yeah," I said, taking the bottle from him. "I guess you are at that."

"When do we leave?"

"The day after Jenny gets in touch again," I told him.

Now he shook his head. "You mean you still plan on taking her along?"

"She wants out, Bags, so I'm taking her out. We're just acting as escort that's all. You wouldn't want to see the Comanches get a hold of her, would you?"

"I guess not, but her old man isn't going to take kindly to her leaving with you," he told me. Then his face brightened, as if he'd just realized something.

"Damn, but you're sneaky," he told me.

"What do you mean?"

"You got it figured, from start to finish, ain't you? You take her with you, Soto's got to send Melendez and some others after us. That's how you plan on taking care of that big Mex foreman."

Actually, the thought had never entered my mind, but when I thought about it, he was right. Soto wasn't just going to let Jenny leave, and if she was gone, and I was gone, he'd put two and two together. He'd either send Melendez after us, or come himself.

"So that takes care of Melendez," Bags said, "but what about Soto? What's your plan for him?"

"I don't have any plans for anybody but me, Bags. I'll let you know when we're leaving."

"Okay, okay, you want to play it that way, fine. Don't let me in on your plans," he sulked, pouring himself another drink. "I'll find out when the time comes."

"Yeah," I said, standing up, "we'll both find out when the time comes."

"Sure, pard, sure."

I dropped two bits on the table. "Finish the bottle. I'm going for a walk."

"See you later."

So I left one stray in the cantina, while the other one got up off the floor and followed me out. It seemed as if I was specializing in picking up strays lately, and Jenny looked like she was going to be stray number three.

I went down to the livery to sit with Duke. I did that a lot when I wanted to think. I thought about my rig, which I had left back in Texas, and hoped that it was in one piece. I thought about my rep, which Joe Bags envied so much. It was a mixed reputation, the kind Wakeman didn't like. I had never thought about it much myself, but I did just then.

I was proud of my reputation as a lawman, but I admitted that very often I'd ended up enforcing the law with my gun, and that had given rise to my second reputation, as a gunman. Now, I had never been ashamed of my abilities with a gun, and I really didn't think I had any reason to be ashamed of the way I had used it over the years, so why were Wakeman's words bothering me?

Why was I depressed as hell and feeling ornery?

Leaving Blessed Gate—and Mexico—was the only way I could think of to relieve my depression. Leaving without Jenny would have been ideal, but could I walk away and forget about her? Or would I be looking for her again in thirteen years, just to close an open chapter in my life?

No, the best way for me to close this chapter for good was to see her safely out of Mexico to wherever she wanted to go, then pick up my rig and pick up my life from where I had left off.

36

A message came from Jenny two days later. It said I was to meet her on Soto land, by that same clump of trees where Melendez and his men had jumped me before.

Another trap? I couldn't afford to take the chance.

"What are you, crazy?" Bags asked when I told him that we were close to leaving.

"No," I said, coldly. "I'll meet Jenny and set it up for her to meet us tomorrow."

"You're gonna get your head kicked in again," he told me. "At least let me ride by there first and check it out."

"No. Just do what I tell you."

"Clint, you've got to check it out first," he reasoned.

"I will, Bags. Or at least my friend will," I said, pointing at Red. "He tried to warn me last time, but it was too late. I'll send him up ahead. If there's anyone waiting for me there, he'll know it."

"You're gonna depend on that mongrel dog?"

I looked at Red and said, "He's proved himself several times over, Bags. Yeah, I'm going to depend on him."

"It's your head."

"That's right. It's my head."

It was uncanny the way that big red dog understood what I wanted him to do. As we approached that rise

189

with the clump of trees, he took off ahead of Duke and me, circled the trees a few times, then ran back us. He didn't appear to be particularly agitated, and after what happened to him the last time, I was sure that meant no one was around. If there had been, he would have been going crazy.

When I reached the trees I verified that no one was around, not even Jenny. Just to be on the safe side, I walked Duke out of sight among the trees and waited there for Jenny to show.

When she did, she came from the opposite direction, as I had expected. I waited until she had almost reached us, and when I was sure she hadn't been followed, I stepped out from the trees.

She rode up, dismounted and tied off her horse.

"I couldn't make it to the hotel, Clint," she told me, "so I figured this was the next best place. They wouldn't expect us to meet here again."

"Have you had trouble?"

"Some, yes," she said. "Manuel has insisted that I not go out at night, but he has continued to allow me to take my morning ride."

"Okay, then we'll play it this way, Jenny. Tomorrow you take your morning ride, but be ready to travel. Meet us here—"

"Us?" she asked.

"There's someone riding with us, but he's all right."

"All right."

"Meet us here and we'll leave immediately. I'll get all the supplies we'll need. All you'll need are some clothes, and your horse. Don't take too much stuff, or he'll get suspicious."

"Clint, when he realizes that I'm gone, he'll know I've left with you. He'll come after us."

In spite of myself I thought briefly of unpaid debts.

"Will he send Melendez?"

"He'll go with him," she told me. "Manuel is still a very active man—in some ways."

"Do you still want to go?" I asked.

"Yes," she said without hesitation. "It's a decision I'm years late in making."

"Where will you go?"

"San Francisco," she answered, as if she had it all planned out in advance.

"Why Frisco?"

"It's big, it's busy. I'm tired of small towns, Clint. I want to go to a large city, where it's so busy I'll have less time to think—and regret."

I nodded, not wanting to get into a discussion about her regrets.

"What about Angie?" I asked.

"What about her?"

"Will she be a problem?"

"Why should she?"

"Well, since we've begun being totally honest with each other," I said, "Angie has some ideas about, uh—"

"You and her?"

"Uh—yes."

She thought a moment.

"Angie—as you call her—is young, but she's still a woman," she told me.

"I noticed."

"I'm sure," she said. "Angel has always been vindictive."

"So, if she gets the chance, she'll try to hurt me."

She nodded. "And if she can hurt *me* at the same time, all the better," she added.

"I guess we'll just have to watch our step, then."

"You don't have to do this, you know, Clint," she said, giving me an out.

"Oh, I think I do, Jenny—and for selfish reasons."

"Whatever your reasons are, I'm grateful."

We stared at each other for a few awkward moments, and then she stepped close to me and said, "I don't suppose we could . . ."

We went into the cover of the tree and undressed. The coupling was quick and frenzied, but satisfying for both of us. I traced her neck and her breasts with my lips, and then I was atop her and inside. She thrust her hips up off the ground to meet my thrusts, and moments later gave a small scream of completion.

"It's too bad we aren't in love," she said later, as we dressed.

"We were once," I told her.

"But not enough I guess, or else you wouldn't have left, and neither would I."

In spite of my efforts to ignore them, we had gotten around to her regrets, anyway.

"There's no point in going over old mistakes," I told her.

"No, I suppose not," she said. "Not when we're about to make new ones."

On that cheery thought she mounted her horse.

"I'll meet you here at first light," she told me.

"Be careful, Jenny."

She smiled.

"I haven't been called that for years."

"I'll see you tomorrow."

I watched her until she disappeared beyond the rise, then mounted Duke and headed back to town.

New mistakes, she had said. And she was probably right.

37

"I'll be leaving in the morning," I told the desk clerk, "and I'd like to settle my bill now."

After we had taken care of that I asked, "Are there any messages for me?"

He checked, and came up with the one Angie had left days ago.

"I am sorry, Señor, that it is so late—" he began.

"Don't worry," I told him. "It's my own fault. Thank you, anyway."

I went upstairs and got my gear packed, then went out looking for Bags. I found him out in back of the cantina, playing with his gun.

"How did your meeting go?" he asked. "Any new lumps?"

"Not a one. We'll meet Jenny there at first light tomorrow, and be on our way. Settle up your hotel bill. I've taken care of mine already."

"All right."

He reloaded his Colt, then looked at me.

"I've been wondering," he said.

"What?"

"I've been wondering how fast I really am with this," he said, indicating the Colt.

"So?"

"So, there are two bottles left on that fence," he went on, pointing to them. "Why don't you take one and I'll take the other."

"I don't draw my gun to play games, Bags," I told him. "I don't consider them play things."

"Oh, really? According to your rep—"

"Bags, I think that if you mention my *rep* one more time—"

"Okay, okay," he said, holding up his hands. He looked at his right hand, as if just discovering he was holding his gun. He lowered his hand and fanned his gun twice, shattering both bottles, then returned it to his holster.

"Let's get a drink," he said.

He was a cocky young man, proud of his ability with a gun. I liked him—maybe less than before, but I liked him. I was, however, starting to question his motives for dogging my trail the way he was. If Soto and Melendez came after us, though, I knew he'd be handy to have along, so I decided to take the good with the bad—at least for now.

"Okay," I said, "but you buy."

"Sure."

He started to walk past me to the door and I put a hand on his arm.

"What?"

"Don't forget to reload that gun."

He looked sheepish and reloaded it as we walked back into the cantina.

Inside we found the sheriff waiting for us at a table with three drinks set out. We looked at each other, Bag and I, then walked to where the lawman was seated.

"What's this about?" I asked.

He spread his hands expansively and said, "Just a little farewell drink, to show there's no hard feelings."

Bags and I swapped looks again, then I nodded an

we sat down. "You leave instructions with the clerk at the hotel to let you know when I settled my bill?"

"Uh-huh. You've done that yourself, I'd bet."

"Once or twice," I admitted, "in special cases."

"And you're a special case," he told me. He raised his drink and added, "A safe trip to . . . to . . . where are you headed, anyway?"

I shrugged, picking up my drink.

"A safe trip," I said, "to wherever."

He matched my shrug and said, "To wherever."

We all drank up, and then he got to his feet.

"Oh, Sheriff?" Bags called.

"Yeah?"

"Anymore accidents out at Rancho Soto?"

Wakeman gave him a hard look and said, "No, not so far. Why?"

"Well, I used to work with those guys. I'm concerned."

"Yeah," Wakeman said, looking at me, "I know."

He walked out and it was my turn to give Bags a hard look.

"You've got to learn," I told him, "who to play cute with, and who not to play cute with. You don't fence with men like Wakeman, Bags. Remember that."

"Yes, Papa."

He stood up and I said, "Where are you going?"

"To get another drink."

"Forget that. Settle your bill, then check your horse. Make sure he's fit to travel."

"And then?"

"And then make one last visit to Rosa's. Get enough to hold you for a while. We'll be on the move for some time."

"You mean, with the lady along you ain't gonna share?"

"Bags—"

"Okay, I'm sorry, I didn't mean it," he said, holding both hands out at me, palms showing. "I'm going, I'm going."

Yeah, I thought as he walked out, a cocky kid, and getting cockier. Maybe too cocky.

38

I picked up all the supplies we could carry on our horses without needing a pack animal and brought them to the livery. We were going to have to be able to travel fast, and pack animals would slow us down. Bags may have wanted to be caught by Soto and Melendez, but I'd decided to stay as far ahead of them as possible.

"Make this up into three equal bundles," I told Tico. Jenny was going to have to carry her weight if she wanted to come with us, and I felt sure that would be the way she wanted it.

"Three bundles?" a voice asked from behind me. I turned and saw Angie standing by the door.

"I saw you come out of the general store and followed you over here," she told me. "Were you going to leave without saying goodbye?" she asked.

"I couldn't very well ride up to your ranch to say goodbye," I told her. "Your father wouldn't have liked that much."

"Uh-huh." She looked past me at Tico and asked me, "Why do you need three bundles?"

"I'm not traveling alone," I told her.

"You're taking her with you, aren't you?"

"Who?"

"You know who. Jennifer."

"Angie—"

"Don't worry," she said, "I am glad she is going. I never approved of her marriage to my father. I am glad she is going away with you."

"Angie, she's not going away with me. She is only traveling with us."

"Us?"

"A friend named Joe Bags is riding along, too."

"Bags?" she said, the name striking a cord. "One of my father's hands?"

"He was until he was fired."

"Oh, I remember that. I never knew why he was fired, though. My father would not tell me."

"Well, he got fired for being my friend."

"I see."

I turned to see how Tico was doing, and he was almost done.

"I hope you know my father will come after you," she told me.

"You mean he'll come after her."

She shrugged.

"If she is with you it will be the same thing. I hope Joe Bags is also prepared to die for being your friend."

"Angie, tell me about your father."

"What is there to tell? He is a possessive man, Clint. He will not stand still while something he owns is taken away—or even tries to walk away on its own."

Which meant there was no doubt that he'd come after us once he discovered we were gone.

"Do you love her, Clint?" she asked.

"No, I don't love her."

She touched my arm and asked, "Why are you risking your life, then?"

"We're old friends, Angie. She wants to get out, and I'm helping her, that's all."

Now she began rubbing my arm, saying, "You could

stay here with me, Clint. I could make Father accept you."

"From what I know about Emmanuel Soto, no one can make him do anything he doesn't want to do. What you said about him backs that up." I took her hand off my arm and held it. "I don't love Jenny, Angie, and I don't love you either."

For a moment that vindictive little girl Jenny had spoken about put in an appearance on Angie's face, and then it was gone.

"I'm sorry, Angie," I added, letting her hand go. "Now, if we get a big enough head start on your father, he won't catch us. If he does catch us, anything can happen, Angie." I was trying to erase any ideas she may have had about going to him and telling him. "A lot of people could end up getting killed, including your father."

"I understand. When are you leaving?"

"I haven't decided yet."

She gave me a look, and then looked at Tico, who was finishing up the bundles.

"You wouldn't be packing unless you were leaving early in the morning, Clint," she told me.

"Angie—"

She didn't look vindictive anymore, but a look crossed her face that I didn't quite trust. I wished I could get word to Jenny to meet us tonight.

"Clint, I won't tell my father," she promised. "I'm glad I saw you so I could say goodbye, though."

"So am I."

"Vaya con dios," she said. She reached up and kissed me quickly on the mouth, and then she was gone.

"Señor," Tico called from behind me, "I am finished."

I turned and looked at him, standing over three bundles of supplies, and said, "Yeah, I think I am, too."

39

"If I could find out how she got her messages to me," I told Bags, "I could get a message to her the same way."

"So, how do we find out?"

"I'll find out. You check out your horse—like you were supposed to do before," I told him.

"Well," he said, looking sheepish, "I had to pass Rosa's on the way to the livery, and you did tell me to get as much as I could—"

"Right, I did. Okay, go over to the livery, check out your horse, because if I can get a message to Jenny, we'll be leaving tonight."

"If she tries to leave the house tonight, her husband is gonna catch on right quick," he said.

"I know, but in the dark they'll have a hard time tracking us, so they still might not start out until morning."

"Okay, good luck."

I went over to the hotel and talked to the hotel clerk.

"Señor?"

"What's your name?" I asked him.

"My name is Roberto, Señor."

"Roberto, I've been getting some messages here for the past few weeks, and I was wondering if you could tell me who has been bringing them here."

I knew I'd hit paydirt right off when he looked down at the top of the desk.

"Roberto?"

"Si, Señor?"

"You do know, don't you?"

"I am not supposed to say, Señor."

I took out a dollar and put it down on the desk top. He looked at it longingly, then looked at me with sad eyes.

"It is a family thing, Señor. I cannot."

I leaned on the desk and said, "Roberto, I can either take out another dollar, or I can take out my gun. If I were you I'd pick up this dollar."

His eyes were no longer sad, they were frightened. He picked up the dollar from the counter and said, "Si, Señor. What is it you wish to know?"

It turned out that Roberto's cousin, Rosita, worked for the Señora Soto, and it was she who had been bringing the messages for her cousin to put in my box.

"Could she bring a message to the Señora for me?" I asked.

He shrugged a bit helplessly and said, "I could ask her, Señor, but—"

"Ask her," I told him. "Give me a paper and pencil."

I wrote Jenny a note, telling her to meet us at the same place, but at midnight, not at first light.

I gave it to him, with another dollar.

"Give the note and the dollar to your cousin. Tell her I want the note delivered tonight. If this is done, I will give you each five dollars more. Comprende?"

"Sir, comprendo, Señor. It will be done."

"I'll be in my room. Let me know if it isn't done."

"It will be done, Señor."

I tapped the note in his hand and said, "Make sure she knows that no one else must see that, Roberto. No one."

"Seguro, of course, Señor."

"Gracias."

I went up to my room and waited. Eventually there was a knock on the door and it was a young girl wearing a shawl over her head and shoulders.

"Señor Adams?"

"Yes."

"I have a note for you," she told me, handing it to me. I opened it and read it. It said simply: "Midnight."

"Roberto said you would give me cinco dolares."

I took it out and gave it to her.

"And for my cousin?"

"No offense, Señorita, but I will give your cousin's money to your cousin."

She nodded and went off down the hall.

I put Jenny's note in my pocket, grabbed my hat and went looking for Bags.

At the livery Tico told me Bags had been there checking his horse, but that he was gone now.

"Is his horse fit to travel?" I asked.

"Si, Señor. He is not a Duke, but he is a nice caballo."

"Good. Thanks, Tico."

"Por nada, Señor."

Bags had to be either in the bar, or at Rosa's. Knowing him, I checked the whorehouse first.

When I walked into Rosa's I noticed right off that the place was too quiet. I walked through the entry hall to the sitting room and found out why.

Apparently Bags and another man took a fancy to the same girl, and both were claiming her. They were facing each other, both on their feet, and I couldn't tell if they were going to slug it out, or go for their guns.

Bags looked relaxed, an amused look on his face. The other man was bigger and older and had his back to me. His shoulders were of an impressive width, and his hands were very large, clenching and unclenching at his sides.

"I'm telling you, amigo," Bags said to him, "there's plenty of señoritas down here for you to pick from. Gracie is kind of my favorite, you know? There's no reason for you to die over a piece of tail."

"Caramba," the man snapped. "I have her first, she is mine!"

"Mister, you asked for it. You can go for your gun anytime—"

"No," the big man said. His hands disappeared in front of him and he unbuckled his gunbelt and threw it aside. "No guns. We will fight like men."

The amused look disappeared from Bags's face. Apparently he didn't consider himself to be as good with his hands as he was with his guns. I leaned up against the wall to watch.

"Look, compadre, you're a little bigger than I am—"

"Hijo de un cabron," the man snapped, "you are a coward, then?"

"Shit," Bags said. He swept his hat off with his right hand as if to throw it aside, then with a flick of his wrist he snapped the hat into the big man's face. The big man flinched, and Bags followed it up with a right hand to the jaw. I saw the big man's head snap back. Bags looked at the man as if he expected him to fall down, and then the big man's right arm described a back-handed arc that ended on Bags face. Bags was thrown literally off his feet and into the chair, which turned over with the force of his landing. When he peeked up from behind the overturned chair there was blood coming from his mouth.

"Bit off a little more than you could chew, huh?" I asked Bags.

His eyes flicked past the big man to me, and then a wide smile creased his face.

"Well, well, am I glad to see you," he said.

"Why's that?"

"Because now I don't have to fight him," he told me.

"You think I'm going to fight your battles for you?" I asked.

"Not mine," he said. "Yours."

"What are you talking about, Bags? C'mon, get up and take your licking like a man."

He shook his head and stood up, still smiling.

"Hey, amigo," he said to the big man, "do me a favor and turn around, will you?"

"Porque?" the man asked.

"Just do it," Bags said, making circles with his index finger, "just turn around for a minute."

"Bags, you're—" I started to say, but then the big man did turn around and look at me, and I saw his face.

It was Melendez, the foreman of Rancho Soto.

40

"See what I mean?" Bags asked, but I barely heard him. My reaction to Melendez's presence baffled even me. A loud roar started up in my head, and I remembered the pain in my shoulder as my wound split open. Most of all, though, I remembered his voice as he called for his men to shoot Red, and he was lucky that I had left Red outside when I came in.

"Pick up your gun, Melendez," I told the big Mexican.

His mouth split into a wide grin—only his wasn't the same type of grin as Bags's. Melendez had a vicious, malicious grin.

"No," the big foreman said, turning to face me, "you will fight me as a man, even if your friend would not. You will not shoot me while I am not wearing a weapon."

His big hands were flexing open and closed and he watched me carefully as I unbuckled my gunbelt and set it aside on a chair.

I took off my hat and dropped it very deliberately on the floor at my feet.

"Come, gringo," he told me, beckoning me with his big hands, "I will make little pieces out of you."

He would too, if I wasn't careful, extremely careful. I

began to circle to my right, and the girls and other customers in the place all huddled together in one corner of the room. Bags had righted the chair he'd flipped over and was sitting in it with his legs crossed, watching.

I decided to wait the big man out and let him make the first move. I thought I had more patience, and more speed.

After a few moments of circling, he was growing impatient, and finally moved in. I flicked out a quick left jab which caught him on the nose, than backed away as he grabbed for me. While he was off balance from the missed grab I stepped in again and threw a hard right, again hitting him on the nose. He howled with pain and grabbed for his nose.

When he did that I threw two right hands into his belly, but that was futile. He had a large belly, but it was hard as a rock, and my blows had no effect. I had also underestimated his speed, because he brought one hand away from his nose and threw a backhand, which I caught part of. It made my ears ring and stunned me long enough.

He lowered his head and charged. I tried to back away, but I banged into the wall and then he had me. He scooped me up in his arms and started applying pressure with a monstrous bearhug. I could feel my back creaking and I knew right away there was no way I could force his arms open. Since his nose appeared his weak spot, I drew my head back and brought it forward as hard as I could. When my forehead made contact with his nose I felt it break and I felt his blood on my face as it spurted.

His cry of pain and outrage filled the room and instead of tightening his hold on me he threw me across the room. Lucky for me I landed on the couch, which flipped over, depositing me on the floor.

When I looked up Melendez was standing in the cen-

ter of the room like a great grizzly. The blood was leak-
ing from his face and by rubbing at it he had gotten it in
his eyes. For all intents and purposes, at that moment he
was blind and I was quick to seize the opportunity.

Feeling no shame whatsoever, I walked up to the big
man and kicked him in the cojones. He opened his
mouth to scream and no sound came out, although the
cords on his neck were standing out. With his mouth
open like that it quickly caught some of the blood from
his nose and he started to choke on it. He didn't know
what to do first, grab himself where I kicked him, or try
to clear his mouth and throat. Whichever it was, he had
to bend over to do it, and when he did I drew my boot
back and kicked him in the head.

He toppled over like a felled redwood and didn't
move again.

Bags got up from his chair, walked over to Melendez's
inert form and checked him. He stood up and, smiling at
me, said, "He's still alive."

I walked up to him, drew my fist back and hit him a
shot that knocked him back into and over the same
chair as before.

He looked up at me from over the fallen chair, blood
on his mouth again, and said, "Jesus, what'd you do
that for?"

I had to get my breath back before I spoke, and when
I finally did I told him, "I had one left."

41

It was after eleven when we left Rosa's and I took Bags directly to the livery to saddle his horse.

"I got stuff at the hotel," he complained.

"Anything you can't do without?" I asked.

"Well, no—"

"Good. Saddle up, I want to get out of town before Melendez wakes up, and before the sheriff finds out what happened. We'll ride out to the meeting place and wait there for Jenny."

"You got a message to her?" he asked.

"I did. She'll meet us there."

"It's still your show."

We stopped outside the livery to wash our faces in the horse trough, and then went in to saddle up. Red was prancing around, sensing a long trip ahead. Or maybe he was just as anxious to get out of Blessed Gate as I was.

"I will be sorry to see this magnificent animal leave my place, Señor Adams," Tico told me.

"Well, you've taken good care of him for me, Tico. I appreciate it," I told him, handing him some bills.

"Gracias, Señor," he said, looking at the money. "It was my great pleasure."

I tied my gear, which I had brought over with the

supplies, to my saddle, then took one of the three bundles of supplies and tied that on, too.

I picked up a second bundle and threw it to Bags.

"Tie that on. I'll carry the third until we meet Jenny."

"Gonna make her pull her own weight?" he asked, smiling.

"Everybody is going to pull their own weight," I told him.

"Well, if she gets tired, I'll offer to help," he said. He turned to tie the supplies to his saddle, so he missed my dirty look.

When we reached the meeting point we dismounted and led the horses out of sight under the trees, then sat on the ground to wait.

"What if she doesn't show?" he asked.

"She will."

"How long should we give her?"

"Until she shows."

"And what if she doesn't show?"

I looked at him.

"Clint, be reasonable. We've got to set a time limit just in case something goes wrong."

It only took me a couple of seconds to admit he was right.

"All right. She's supposed to meet us at midnight. We'll give her half an hour beyond that, and then we'll leave without her."

"Okay."

At about twelve-fifteen we heard the sound of a horse.

"How many?" he asked, getting to his knees.

I listened for a moment, then said, "I make it one."

"So do I."

Nevertheless, we stayed out of sight until we were sure that it was Jenny, and she was alone.

"What the hell is that?" Bags asked.

"Shit," I said.

Bags had been the one who told me that Soto had a stallion that he was proud of, but he hadn't told me that it was a palomino.

"She's got Soto's stallion, man," Bags told me.

"I see."

She rode up on us, stopped and dismounted, holding on tight to the reins.

"What the hell are you doing with that horse?" Bags asked her before I could speak.

She looked at both of us with wide eyes, apparently wondering what she had done wrong.

"I needed a good horse, didn't I?" she asked with infallible feminine logic. "This was the best one on the ranch."

Bags and I just exchanged glances at that, because how could you argue with her? Seeing that animal, I had to admit that it very probably was the finest horse on the ranch.

"Clint, you know Soto's gonna come after that horse," Bags told me. "Excuse me, lady, but even if he don't want his wife back, he's gonna come after that horse."

"I know," I told him. "There's nothing we can do about it now."

"Like hell there ain't. Leave her and the horse right here."

"Clint—" she said, but I waved her quiet.

"Bags, I thought you were the man who wanted Soto to follow us."

He opened his mouth to say something and then couldn't think of anything to say and closed it.

I went up to the stallion and patted him on the nose, and then the neck. No doubt about it, he was a beauty, and he was probably fast, too. In spite of the situation, I had to wonder what the outcome would be in a confrontation between him and Duke.

"Has he got a name?" I asked.

Jenny obviously didn't know, because she started to shake her head, but Bags said, "Prince," in a disgusted voice.

"Hi, Prince, boy," I said, patting his nose again. "He's a beautiful animal, all right."

"I'm sorry, Clint—" she began.

"Don't worry about it. He's a good animal, we'll make good time with him." I turned to Bags and asked, "Will your roan be able to keep up?"

He looked at me indignantly and said, "Just don't worry about my roan, Adams. If we're gonna go, let's go."

"Mount up, Jenny. The man wants to go."

So we went.

42

With a full moon out we made good time riding that night. To Jenny's credit she never asked to rest; with the animal she had under her, she never had to.

Duke reacted to Prince in a way I've never seen him react. I mean, he stood straighter and kept his head high and looked straight ahead. That palomino's name might have been Prince, but Duke was acting like royalty too.

"He can't hold a candle to you, big boy, don't worry," I told him at one point, but that didn't appease him. The bunching of his muscles underneath me was telling me, Let me prove it.

I kept a tight rein on Duke the whole time, because we didn't need any kind of speed duel developing between those two.

By first light we had made up half the distance between Blessed Gate and the border.

"Let's take a break," I announced, and received no argument.

"Break out some chow?" Bags asked.

"No, we'll just rest. We'll eat later."

I knew Jenny could have used some food, but I was intent on making her pull her own weight. If Bags and I could wait, so could she.

I sat on the rock, watching the direction we had just come from.

"You see the way those two animals react to each other?" Bags asked me, indicating Duke and Prince. I had positioned Duke so that Bags's roan stood between him and the palomino. Still, they looked like two bulls measuring each other.

"Yeah, I've noticed."

"When we get out of Mexico, maybe we can let them go at each other," he suggested, "you know, in a race."

"Bags, I treat my horse the way I treat my gun. I never play with either one."

He just shook his head at me and went over to his roan.

Jenny came over and sat next to me.

"Why did you change our plans?" she asked.

"Angie came to see me last night and told me she knew you were leaving with me. She also told me she wouldn't tell her father."

"You didn't believe her."

"No, I didn't."

"How much of a head start do you think we have?" she asked.

"I don't know. Not as much as we would have had if you hadn't taken that horse along."

"I knew I needed a good horse—"

"C'mon, Jenny, you knew how your husband felt about that horse. You must have."

She stared ahead of her for a few moments, then said, "All right, so I knew how he felt. Maybe I just wanted to hurt him."

"Wouldn't leaving him hurt him?" I asked.

"Not as much as losing that horse will."

"He hasn't lost him, yet," I pointed out.

There was another reason she might have taken the horse, one I didn't even want to think about.

She could have wanted her husband to come after us. Why, I didn't know, but I imagined we'd find out if and when he finally did catch up to us.

"Let's get going," I told her. "We've only a couple of hours before we make it to the border." I stood up and called to Bags. He mounted his roan and eased him from between Prince and Duke. I grabbed Duke's reins and walked him away before a confrontation could develop. If the two of them decided to go at each other, there would be little we could do about it. I wasn't about to get between two horses each of which weighed more than twelve hundred pounds.

"Keep your head, big boy, okay?" I asked him, rubbing his nose. He didn't react, which worried me. He always reacted when I spoke to him.

I mounted up and we started out again. I suggested not stopping until we'd crossed the border and they agreed. Once on the Texas side, we'd find somewhere to eat, but after that I didn't want to stop again until we were out of Comanche country. Quanah Parker and the other Comanche chiefs didn't take kindly to white men crossing their land.

As it turned out, worrying about Quanah Parker and the Comanches was counting my chickens before they were hatched.

Bags had the point as we approached the border, and he stopped short when he saw something.

"What's wrong?" I asked, riding up next to him.

He pointed towards the river, and when I looked I saw the problem.

There was a garrison of Mexican soldiers waiting for us at the border. Leading them was one Captain Hernandez who, as I had found out, had recently been promoted to general.

Soto's general!

"Now what?" Bags asked.

Jenny rode up alongside of us and caught her breath.

"Now we go down and see what the head man has to say for himself," I told him.

Bags put his hand on my arm to stop me.

"We could run for it," he suggested.

"Why?" I asked. "And to where?"

He thought it over and then took his hand off my arm.

"Hernandez is in Soto's pocket, Clint," he reminded me, "So don't tell me that the military can't touch us. We've got Soto's wife and his prize stallion."

"Wrong," I told him, "we have Soto's wife *with* us, and *she's* got his stallion. Now let's go see what the man wants."

43

I rode ahead of the others and confronted Hernandez.

"I apologize to you and your party, Señor, but I must detain you," he said.

"Captain!" Jenny called out.

"General," he corrected her.

"General," she conceded, "do you know who I am?"

"Of course, Señora, I am afraid you are the reason I must detain you and your friends."

"For how long?" I asked.

"Until Señor Soto arrives, Señor. Those are my orders. Please make yourselves as comfortable as possible."

"What, no irons?" Bags asked. Hernandez only glanced at him, then wheeled his horse around and approached his men. He let most of them relax, but left about four on horseback in case we made a break, either for the border, or away from it.

"We might as well do as the man says," I told Bags and Jenny.

"Make ourselves comfortable?" Bags asked. "Clint, if we can make it to the Texas side, they can't come after us."

"Sure, Bags, we'll make a break and they'll open fire. With a little luck, our horses will make it to the Texas side, but we sure as hell won't be on them."

I dismounted and led Duke to a shady spot beneath a

tree. Jenny and Bags exchanged glances, and then followed.

"We might as well break out some grub," I told
them.

"How long do you think we'll have to wait?" Jenny
asked.

"Few hours maybe."

"How the hell did they get here so fast?" Bags wondered.

"Telegraph. Soto probably sent a message to
Hernandez to meet us here."

"How did they know where we'd cross?"

"He probably had them all covered."

"And we happened to pick the one Hernandez was
waiting at?"

"We picked the best spot to cross," I told him.

Building a fire would have been making ourselves too
much at home, so we settled for jerky and cold beans.

"I feel like a target waiting for someone to be shot
at," Bags complained.

"You've shot at enough targets in your day," I told
him. "Now you know how they feel."

"Ha ha."

He got up and began to pace back and forth, which
made some of the soldiers nervous. I wondered if they
had any idea why we were being detained. I only hoped
none of them got trigger happy, thinking they were
guarding some political criminals.

"Clint, what's going to happen?" Jenny asked.

"Well, your husband will come, and you'll talk to
him. If that doesn't work, I'll talk to him."

"And if that doesn't work?"

I looked at her and shrugged.

"We'll just have to wait and see, Jenny."

We didn't have to wait long. We all became aware of
approaching horses at the same time. When they appeared there were about eight riders. I recognized Soto,

and Melendez, whose face was bandaged. The rest were probably just hands.

"They haven't disarmed us," said Bags.

"You want to start shooting?" I asked him. "See how far that gets us."

"We've got to do something."

"Sit tight, Bags, just sit tight. If there's any shooting to be done, I'll fire the first shot. From then on, you're on your own."

The three of us stood up as Soto and his men approached. They rode right past us, and Soto never turned his head. He rode up to Hernandez and dismounted. They talked for a few moments, then Soto pointed in our direction and Hernandez nodded.

When he came over Hernandez said, "Señor Adams, the patron—ah, Señor Soto would like to speak with you."

I looked at Bags and Jenny.

"I guess now is when we find out what's what," I said.

I followed Hernandez to where Soto was standing, and then the Mexican General stood off to the side.

"Señor Adams, you have taken something that belongs to me," Soto told me.

I shook my head.

"I have not taken your wife, Señor Soto, I am simply escorting her."

He waved in hand in annoyance and said, "I am not speaking of my wife, Señor. You have taken my prize stallion."

"You're wrong again, Soto," I told him. "Your wife took your prize stallion. Take that up with her. My friend and I simply want to cross the border. Why don't you and your wife discuss your problems? If she still wants to leave Mexico, we'd be more than happy to see her safely to a town in Texas."

He smiled wanly and said, "Do you really expect me to believe that she was not going away with you?"

"Believe what you like, Señor, but I am telling you the truth," I told him.

He shook his head a couple of times, then snapped something in Spanish to the general. Hernandez then called out in Spanish and he and his men pulled their guns. I could have cleared leather before he did, but it wouldn't have done any good. I hoped Bags had enough sense to lay off his iron as well.

"I am afraid, Señor, that we must treat you as common horse thieves. You and your friend will hang, and my wife will of course accompany me home."

"What are you going to do, Soto, put her under twenty-four-hour guard?"

"My marital affairs are of no concern to you, Señor," Soto told me. "I attempted to explain this to you some weeks ago, but you chose not to listen." He waved his arm at Hernandez and said, "Andale."

They still hadn't taken my gun, and I suspected that they were hoping I would go for it so they could simply shoot us down and be done with it. For once Bags seemed to have listened to what I said, because he was still waiting for me to go for mine first.

A couple of soldiers flanked me and they each grabbed an arm and marched me back to Bags and Jenny, where two soldiers were similarly holding him.

"Why haven't they taken our guns?" Bags asked.

"They want us to draw so they can shoot us down."

"And if we don't?"

"They're going to hang us."

"Shit, I'm reachin' for mine," he said.

"No, not yet," I told him.

"Better gettin' shot than hung," he snapped.

"Better neither," I told him. "Jenny, how good is that palomino?"

"Manuel says there isn't a horse in the world who can touch him," she told me.

"Great," I said, but it was worth a try.

They were getting two horses ready and a rope for each of us.

"Just follow my lead," I told Bags.

"Shit."

It was at that moment that I noticed something strange. Red was nowhere to be seen.

"Where's the dog?" I asked Bags.

"What? They're fixing to hang us and you're worried about your dog?"

"Where the hell is he?" I wondered aloud.

The soldiers holding us walked us over to where the ropes were waiting. Melendez was staring at me malevolently, standing by a horse I knew would be mine. He wanted to be the one to slap it out from under me.

Soto was close by, within earshot, so as the soldiers walked me to the horse, I said, "Jesus, all this fuss over a horse that couldn't even keep up with mine from Blessed Gate to here."

"Basta!" he shouted, and all movement stopped.

He approached me and stood face to face.

"Señor, what was that remark you made about my Prince?"

I shrugged.

"Nothing much. I was just wondering why you were fussing over him. He don't seem like nothing special to me."

"Caramba, nothing special? Señor, you are no judge of horse flesh."

I laughed.

"No judge of horse flesh. Look at my animal, Señor Soto, and tell me I am no judge of horse flesh."

He looked over at Duke, then back at me.

"I admit, Señor, that he is impressive to look upon, but size is not everything."

"Neither are pretty colors," I told him. "Your animal's got nice golden flesh, and a fair mane, sure.

He'd make a good show horse, but he can't be much use beyond that. I had to keep slowing Duke down so that palomino could catch up."

"Impossible. There is no horse alive that can outrun Prince," he announced.

"Mine can," I told him.

He stared at me hard, then said something to the two men holding me, who then released me.

"I'll make a bargain with you," I told him. "No, make that a wager."

"Continue."

"My horse against your horse in a race. If I win, you let us go, and your wife, if she wishes. We will take our horses, and you can keep Prince. Just supply us with another mount for Jennifer."

"And if you lose?"

"You can hang us."

He thought a moment. "I could hang you anyway, Señor," he pointed out.

"I think you are a man of your word, Señor," I told him, hoping I was right. "If you say you will let us go, I will believe you."

"How much of a distance will be involved in this race?" he asked.

"May I?" I asked, indicating I wanted to move around.

"Please," he said, and then gave instructions in Spanish, I suppose so no one would interfere with my movements.

I walked to the river's edge and looked up and down, seeking some kind of landmark. About a hundred yards one way was a tall tree that had recently died. It was barren and easily recognizable.

"That tree," I told him, pointing. He came alongside of me to see where I was pointing. "We'll ride to it, around it and back again. First one back is the winner."

He thought it over and then said, "Bueno. It will be done."

"You agree to the terms of the wager?" I asked.

"I agree. You have my word."

"Good. Who will ride for you?" I asked.

He stood up ramrod straight and said, "I will ride Prince myself, Señor. There is no better horseman in all of Mexico."

I believed him.

He walked back to Hernandez and Melendez and explained the wager to them. Hernandez shrugged fatalistically, figuring that whatever the patrone wanted was fine with him. Melendez, on the other hand, began to argue with him, and was cut short by a quick barrage of words. The big foreman stared over at me, wishing me all the bad luck in the world.

I went and got Duke and walked him to the makeshift starting line.

"You been wanting this for a while, big boy, and now you've got your chance. Don't let me down."

Duke pawed the ground, as if telling me he was ready to go.

Soto brought Prince to the starting line, and it was amazing the way neither animal looked at the other.

The soldiers, Soto's men, and Jenny and Bags formed a line that stretched half the distance of the race. Hernandez was the starter. We mounted up and kept our eyes on him.

The general took out his gun, pointed it in the air, and fired.

That palomino took off like a shot and right off I knew I'd made a mistake.

The mistake was setting the race up so close to the shore of the river. The sand was wet and, with Duke's extra size and weight, he sank into it deeper than the other horse. Duke's weight was also against us. Because of it Duke would take longer to get rolling. By the time he did, we'd be at that tree and have to go around it, and then he'd have to get himself rolling again. I only hoped there was enough distance for him to do it.

That golden stallion got a good head start on us, with
Soto using a little whip on his flanks. All I did to Duke
was talk to him the whole time, telling him how much
better he was than the other horse, how much faster he
was than any horse.

As we approached the tree we started to make up
ground on them, but had to slow for the turn. The
stallion went around the tree first, and we followed in
his path, which wasn't easy. He had churned up the mud
some, and Duke sank even deeper.

Now we were straightened out and heading for the
finish line. The men were yelling and screaming, and I
was sure that not all of them were rooting for the
palomino. Some of them would love to see the patrone
get beat.

"We got to do it now, boy," I told Duke. We were
halfway between the tree and the finish line and Duke
was letting it all out. Slipping as he was in the mud, he
was closing the gap between us and the golden horse.
About ten yards from the finish he hooked that horse
neck and neck, eye to eye, and by the time we reached
the finish we had him beat almost a full length.

Money was already exchanging hands, as the men
who'd bet on Duke were collecting from the ones who'd
bet on Prince.

We slowed out horses up and eventually we ended up
riding side by side while we let them wind down.

"That's a nice horse you got there, Señor Soto,"
told him in all honesty. I had never thought there was a
horse alive who could get within a length of Duke.

"Thank you, Señor, but that black giant of yours is
magnificent," he replied with admiration. All the
animosity he'd felt towards me was lost in his admiration for Duke.

My big black was blowing hard, his great lungs heav-
ing beneath me. If not for the mud, we might have
beaten Prince by more, but that took nothing away from

the golden horse. He also had to contend with the mud, and he'd done well.

"You are free to go, Señor," Soto said, "but would you consider selling this great animal?"

"I'm sorry, Señor, I could no more do that than cut off my right arm," I told him.

"I understand," he said. He patted Prince on the neck and spoke to him in Spanish.

"What did you tell him?" I asked.

"I told him that he had nothing to be ashamed of, he was beaten by a black demon."

"That's an awful nice horse, Señor," I said again, "you got a lot to be proud of."

"Gracias."

We were riding back to the crowd when I heard Bags voice suddenly call out, "Clint, watch out."

I tried to locate the danger he was warning me about, but there were too many people milling around. Too late, I saw Melendez aiming his gun at me and knew I wouldn't be able to draw in time.

I didn't have to.

That big red dog came out of nowhere and, ignoring the giant's gun hand, snapped his jaws shut on the foreman's throat. I don't know where he'd been hiding, but he reappeared at just the right time.

The big Mexican went down under Red's weight, but never let go of his gun. He rolled around with Red hanging on, then worked his way to his knees. I jumped off of Duke, still watching as the big man's superior strength started working for him. He worked his left hand up into Red's fur, grabbed a tight hold and yanked. The pain it caused him must have been intense, and bits of flesh went with Red as he flew through the air and landed in the Rio Grande. Melendez was intent on killing me and swung his gun around again, his chest covered with blood from his throat.

"Drop it!" I shouted at him, drawing my gun. The

sound of my voice pinpointed my location for him again and he started to bring his gun to bear. To me he was moving in slow motion, and as he did do I shot him in the forehead, putting him out of his pain and misery.

Some of the soldiers were drawing their guns now, not at all sure what was happening, and Bags drew his and for a moment I thought that was the end.

"Basta!" Hernandez shouted to his men, and when they all looked at him he spoke in rapid Spanish, and they holstered their guns. Bags looked at me and I nodded, holstering mine. The big foreman was the only casualty, and he had brought it on himself.

Soto came up next to me and said, "He was not a man of honor."

"I guess not." I turned to face him and said, "Just out of curiosity, it was Angelique, wasn't it? She told you about us so you had time to telegraph the garrison?"

He shook his head sadly. "I am sorry, Señor, but you are wrong. I did go to the telegraph office to notify General Hernandez as soon as I realized that Prince was gone, but someone had been there ahead of me and already done so."

"Who?"

He looked over at Jenny and it never entered my mind that he might be lying. She had to have taken Prince to be sure Soto would follow, and then used the telegraph to make sure we were caught.

"I will take her back with me and we will discuss this," he told me. "It is obvious to me that she was hoping that you would kill me. If she wishes to go, I will let her go, but with no more than what she came with. If you had checked her saddlebags you would have seen that she took much money and jewelry with her, also. I am afraid that she too is of little honor, Señor."

"Yeah," I replied, "I guess."

TEXAS
1871

44

Jenny couldn't believe it when Bags and I mounted up
and rode into Texas without her. I didn't even look
back, because I was satisfied I'd closed that part of my
past for good, and now could get on with it.

Bags rode with me to the town where I'd left my rig,
a little place called Nolanville. I had decided to rest
Duke over night, after what he'd been through, and go
on in the morning.

In the saloon, I told Bags my plans.

"I'll ride along," he told me.

"No, I don't think so, Bags."

He stared at me hard and asked, "Why not?"

"You make me nervous. I'm not going to be
anybody's reputation-maker. Come morning I'll go my
way and you go yours."

He put his drink down and said, "I can't do that,
Clint. Oh, you're right. I did latch onto you because I
figured that was the surest way to a reputation, but you
were a big disappointment to me. I don't think you're all
that good, after spending so much time with you. You

think too much before drawing your gun, and don't think I believed all that stuff about not playing games with your gun," he told me. "You wouldn't shoot targets with me because you were afraid I'd show you up."

"If that's what you want to believe, Kid, then go ahead," I told him.

"Don't hand me that shit," he snapped, standing up, knocking his chair over. "I'm saying you're yella!"

I had been afraid of this. Realizing that he wasn't going to ride me to a rep, he figured the only other way to get what he wanted was to kill me.

"Don't do this, Bags," I told him. "It's not worth it."

"Outside, Adams, Mr. Gunsmith Clint Adams," he said aloud, making damn sure everyone knew who I was. "I'll be waiting for you outside."

He stormed out of the saloon, leaving me the center of attraction. I finished my drink and then stood up. If I didn't go out and draw on him, he might just kill me anyway. He was that desperate for a "rep." I was going to have to go ahead with this farce, and hope that he was slow enough so that I could take a chance at wounding him. I knew full well I could beat him, I just hoped I could beat him by enough so that I wouldn't have to kill him.

My past was over and done with, all the books were closed, and now I was dealing with the present again.

"Stay here, boy," I told Red, who was sitting under the table. "I'll be right back."

Winners of the SPUR and WESTERN HERITAGE AWARD

☐ 08390	**The Buffalo Wagons**	Kelton	$1.75
☐ 13907	**The Day The Cowboys Quit**	Elmer Kelton	$1.95
☐ 22766	**Fancher Train**	Bean	$1.95
☐ 29742	**Gold In California**	Todhunter Ballard	$1.75
☐ 34272	**The Honyocker**	Giles Lutz	$1.95
☐ 47082	**The Last Days of Wolf Garnett**	Clifton Adams	$1.75
☐ 47493	**Law Man**	Lee Leighton	$1.95
☐ 48921	**Long Run**	Nye	$1.95
☐ 55123	**My Brother John**	Herbert Purdum	$1.75
☐ 56027	**The Nameless Breed**	Will C. Brown	$1.95
☐ 71154	**The Red Sabbath**	Lewis B. Patten	$1.95
☐ 74940	**Sam Chance**	Benjamin Capps	$1.95
☐ 80271	**The Time It Never Rained**	Kelton	$1.95
☐ 82091	**Tragg's Choice**	Clifton Adams	$1.75
☐ 82136	**The Trail to Ogallala**	Benjamin Capps	$1.95
☐ 85904	**The Valdez Horses**	Lee Hoffman	$1.95

Available wherever paperbacks are sold or use this coupon.

Sharp Shooting and Rugged Adventure from America's Favorite Western Writers